Nomad Kind of Love

Prairie Devils MC Romance

Nicole Snow

Description

NOMAD LOVE: OVERWHELMING, FREE, AND UNFORGETTABLE…

June Daniels watched helplessly as the Grizzlies Motorcycle Club destroyed everything she ever cared about. The ruthless gang controls her shattered life, condemning her to darkness without end…until she meets him.

Aaron "Maverick" Sturm doesn't know what it means to settle down. The President of the Prairie Devils Nomads charter is way too hardened, untamable, and dominant for any old lady.

But when he's sent West to establish a new charter, the beautiful woman he takes as collateral from the Grizzlies upends everything. Instincts Aaron never knew existed start to rage, primal desires to love and protect her in his bed, on his bike, and in his heart.

This bad boy loves a challenge. Claiming broken, mysterious June is his fiercest ever.

She can't forsake her need for vengeance on the Grizzlies. He can't let go, even when giving her what she needs most brings savage politics and blood war between MCs.

Will June find love and justice with her outlaw savior – or will her bitter determination ruin the man she loves and his club?

Note: this is a dark and gritty MC romance with language, violence, and love scenes as hard and raw as they come. Outlaw love takes no prisoners!

The Prairie Devils MC books are stand alone novels featuring unique lovers and happy endings. No cliffhangers allowed! This is June and Maverick's story.

I: Broken (June)

To find a knight, first you need a dragon.

My dragon came in columns of snorting engines and leather jackets emblazoned with a roaring bear. It reeked motor oil, cheap tobacco, and hard violence from every savage nook and cranny.

It arrived on the morning of my eighteenth birthday, the day everything I knew and loved was burned to cinders, including my soul.

Rather than becoming a bright young woman, I became a dark shadow.

Lost. Forever broken. Emotionally murdered.

They ruined me, and made me believe I was wrecked beyond redemption. They infected me with their evil, and I waited for it to finish me. Inevitable, right?

I thought so, but then I met *him*...

"What the fuck!"

I jerked up in bed when I heard the words. My father's startled cry shook the entire house.

Clara was rustling beneath me on the bottom bunk, just as rudely awakened as I was, struggling to figure out what was going on.

My ears prickled, and I listened to the conversation just a short walk away.

"Don't act so fucking surprised to see us, Spinner. Did you really think we wouldn't find out?"

A chair was knocked back and hit the floor. My stomach convulsed with terror. I could practically see my father being jerked out of his seat at the kitchen table by some roughneck in leather he called brother.

"Find out what? What the hell are you looking for?" Dad made a noise like he'd been punched. "Oh...you stupid motherfuckers...you think it was me..."

"Let him talk," the gruff voice boomed from the kitchen.

"This is about the shipment that went bad in Boise, yeah? You think I put a fucking bug on it? You think I'd work with pigs? Vulture...*brother*....what gives you the right to break into my own house and call me a fucking rat?"

Deadly silence. Nobody answered my Dad's agonized plea.

Beneath me, Clara sniffed tears sticking her throat. The club had always scared her, and she practically hid whenever the huge, barbaric looking men my father gave his life to showed up to visit.

Then the silence broke. The whole house rattled with the sounds of the kitchen turning upside down, a man struggling, and not very well.

Their numbers subdued him. He never had a chance.

I shook my head, mouthing my worries while the clatter went on.

No, no, no…what the fuck have you gotten yourself into, Dad?

My heart was racing, but my legs still worked. The racket stopped.

The voices were lower, and I climbed down from the bed to get a closer look.

Clara whimpered again behind me. I threw my head over my shoulder and saw her holding up her trembling hands, silently begging me not to open the door.

I did it anyway. I had to know what was going on, what was happening to Dad.

"I didn't fucking do it, Veep! Come on! You've got to believe me. Oh, God…not that. Vulture, you've got nothing. Nothing, and you fucking know it!" Dad's words flitted between horror and defiance.

"Shut the fuck up, rat!" Vulture howled, slamming his fist into soft flesh. "Just shut up a minute. You think we'd break down your fucking door over nothing? How fucking stupid do you think we are, boy?"

Dad snorted. His breathing became a gurgle. I pushed the door open a little more and forced one leg into the hall.

"Nobody rats on the Grizzlies, Spinner. And any bitch who does gets exactly what he deserves." Heavy footsteps fell on the floor as the man spoke, as if he were circling his prey.

"I get it. I really do. You wanted out. You wanted to ride off into the sunset with the family you've neglected for ten years. I can respect that."

"Then…why? Why're you doing this?" Dad's voice sounded shakier than ever. Exhausted. "What the fuck do you want from me?"

"You know nobody leaves this MC alive. There's only one retirement package we offer. And sadly, brother, you don't get any say in it. Not after you ratted out half a mill in smack to the Feds."

Dad screamed again, roaring like a cornered animal, but he was cut off just as fast. More shuffling, boots pounding kitchen tile, and then a sickening crack. Dad's screams were muffled by what sounded like a big block of ice being knocked around in a metal sink.

I gasped. I was frozen in our dingy hallway for what felt like an hour, but it must've been no more than a minute or two.

Adrenaline shot through my system, nearly making me pass out. I forced myself toward the kitchen.

God help me, I did, having a terrible idea what I'd find. The smart thing would've been to stay quiet like Clara wanted.

Unfortunately, my twin sister had the brains in her family. I was just a stubborn bitch, too damned curious for my own good.

Not that it would've saved us.

I realized there was no saving anyone, least of all my father, when I burst in on them. Two greasy men looked up in surprise.

One of them held a dagger in his hands. It dripped the same red gore as the stuff smearing the floor around their feet.

The pair of boots between them was completely limp, the pair belonging to Dad. He was slouched halfway into the sink, head beneath the facet now broken and smeared rusty red.

The third guy, a bigger, even greasier bastard I'd seen before, saw me and smiled.

"Well, if it isn't little Juney Boo-Hoo."

He began moving toward me, too fast and confident for me to turn away. I couldn't do anything except stare at my father's limp body. His blood echoed as it swirled down the drain.

Two goons held him by the shoulders. If they held him up so I could've seen his face, I know I would've screamed at the mangled mess that was left. Steady blood dripped down his sides from where their dagger had torn into him, spilling blood all over the place where we had family dinners a lifetime ago.

"Don't worry, darlin'. This shit with daddy's got nothing to do with you. We're gonna take real good care of you and your Mom."

Vulture clapped me on the shoulder. It wasn't friendly or comforting in any way. His dirty fingers squeezed, a rough pinch twisting my nerves.

I screamed and screamed. Mom came plodding down the hall, rubbing her eyes and pulling on her ratty gown. Clara was right behind her.

"Vulture? What the hell are you doing in my house at the ass crack of –?"

She pushed past me and stopped in her tracks when she saw Dad's body. The thugs holding him shifted their weight uncomfortably. One man released my father's shoulder and he slumped into the sink, like a dummy with its strings cut.

"Holy shit! Holy fuck! What the fuck? George!"

Another hand was on my shoulder, this one nearly as tight as Vulture's. Clara's scream started and almost deafened me. Mom joined us, falling to the floor, tearing at her matted hair as she wept and howled.

"Damn it, we need a little order here!" Vulture roared. "Scoop. Claws. Get your asses over here! Bitch is gonna wake up the dead if she keeps up that shit."

His rough hands found my throat and pushed me to the wall, and then he yanked on Clara's hair. She tried to run, but it was no use.

The men who killed Dad were on her, taking over when their boss released us. They pinned us against the wall, muscular hands like irons we couldn't hope to wriggle out of. Vulture snarled, turning on Mom, who'd crawled across the room and was reaching for Dad's old cell phone near the busted screen door.

"Make sure those little cunts behave! I'll deal with this."

Vulture's boot stomped the phone out of my Mom's fingers. She writhed in pain, falling back and grabbing at her knuckles. He hovered over the phone, slamming his foot on it again and again. Its fragments spiraled into the bloody pools near Dad's limp feet.

"Oh, God. Oh, oh – Jesus!" Mom spat, fell on her side, huddling in a fetal position.

I closed my eyes. Vulture was right over her, and he was going to kick her. I realized for the first time this animal was going to kill my whole family, including me.

"There, there, baby. Everything's gonna be all right, Jenny-Ray. I told you already, my beef's with your asshole old man. Not you and your kids." The evil softness in his voice made my stomach turn. "Lookie, girl. I brought you something to take the edge off…"

The man holding me started to laugh. I opened my eyes, looked past him, and my heart stopped.

Oh, fuck. He thought of everything. It's really over for us now.

Vulture kneeled next to my mother, a nasty smile on his face, holding a small syringe he'd taken from his pocket. He twirled it between his fingers the way a bully would tease a hungry dog with meat.

"You want this, baby? There's plenty more where it came from at the clubhouse. Here, let me slip it in…find a good vein on you." Mom jerked, wrinkling her face with sobs.

Vulture tore her sleeve up and searched her arm. The damage left by old injections was everywhere, but after a few seconds, he slipped the syringe into a fresh channel.

"Nooo Vulture…please…don't hurt me or my kidsss…" Mom's anguish turned to fluffy indifference, and then she slumped on the floor, occasionally twitching while she drooled and giggled.

"Okay. We're done here. Make sure the cleanup guy gets the call before any nosy neighbors come knocking." Vulture stood up.

He looked over his carnage and lit a cigarette, inhaling the smoke deep. Pure bliss painted his face.

"What about them, boss?" The man holding Clara tugged at her hair.

"Get those little sluts on the bikes and make sure they keep their fucking mouths shut. The Missoula clubhouse has been pretty damned light on Prospects lately. Could use a few girls to do the grunge work…maybe even a few new whores. Never had twins before."

He lowered his cigarette and winked at me. That was when I floated back into my body and clenched my jaw, fixing my eyes on this brute, this murderer.

No help was coming. My parents were dead, literally or otherwise, and the police wouldn't find us.

Not here. This was Grizzlies territory, and the minority of cops who weren't paid off stayed away if they wanted to avoid a bullet in the back of the head one quiet night.

Maybe Dad tried to do the right thing. But maybe didn't fucking cut it. If he'd truly helped the Feds, they hadn't given him any protection, or he'd been too damned proud to take it.

He was dead, the badges got what they wanted with the drugs, and they weren't going to bail him out. Clara and I were completely and totally on our own for the first time in our lives.

I raised my head, looking hard at Vulture and his henchmen.

I don't know how or when, but my moment will come. You assholes think I'm a stupid, scared girl from a junkie house. You're right about the junkie part.

But I'm not stupid and I'm not forgiving. One day I'll set this right.

I'll keep Clara safe and bide my time. However long it takes to get out, and then see you as dead as my father.

"Move!" The brute behind me – Claws, I think – pushed his fist into my back. "Don't bite while I get your helmet on and something soft in your mouth. You even think about screaming and we won't hesitate to throw you and your pretty sister off our bikes. Understand?"

I looked up and met his dark eyes. The drying tears on my cheek left hot, rough salt behind.

"Yes, sir. Anything you say."

Scoop, the man with Clara, laughed. "Jesus, that was easy. These girls must be hankering for a little excitement after being cooped up with their shitty parents."

A minute later, we were outside, saddled to the back of their bikes. Clara began to struggle as he gagged her. Scoop spread his palm and smacked her hard across the face.

"Shut up, you whiny little whore. Do yourself a solid and keep quiet like your sister. Struggling's only gonna make this a whole lot worse. Don't believe me, then go ask your old man."

Hatred burned in my belly, and kept burning when they started their bikes. I didn't even look back at my old house one last time.

My old life before that morning receded into dream. Ahead, there was a nightmare, and it was the only thing that mattered besides protecting my sister.

"Juuuuune buuuug!" Vulture roared through the bar. "Hey, where is that piece of shit?"

His buddies laughed. They were drunk off their asses, entertaining some mean looking creep in a suit. He had an accent that sounded Eastern European.

I stayed in the backroom. Sometimes, if I pretended not to hear him, he moved onto the next distraction and forgot about me.

A fresh bottle of Jack or a clubhouse whore to bite and fuck made me disappear real fast. Tonight, though, he was pretty damned persistent.

I thought the Polish man's offerings would've kept them busy tonight. He brought several pretty girls with him who looked even younger than Clara and I.

My sister was in the tiny room we shared, high off weed the new Prospect sold us. It took weeks of scavenging the tips we ferreted away in secret to get a couple joints. Yeah, we should've been using our little stash for better food than the slop they fed us, or maybe for an escape plan.

A car, a hotel, something. We'd been prisoners at the Grizzlies Missoula clubhouse long enough for it to feel like home.

The old life Clara and I knew? A distant memory, if it ever existed at all.

Now there were just days and nights serving these beasts and their buddies. The core members, all ten of them, were usually off doing club business. We tended to their guests when they weren't around. Cooking up burgers, serving drinks, and cleaning bathrooms took up half my reserve energy.

The other half was dedicated to surviving another day intact and sane. Or sane as I could be under these shitty circumstances.

By some sweet miracle, the club hadn't raped me or my sister. Not yet.

But it hung over me, a horrible certainty. I marched to their orders, doing anything they said, just as long as it pushed back our grim fate by a few more hours, days, weeks.

At eighteen, I wasn't a virgin. I had a few messy couplings with boys in high school. Of course, the washouts and junkies I gravitated to in my school's social cliques never interested me much beyond a quick fling.

These men were a different. I wanted to retch every time I thought about their leathery skin wrapped around me. Being forced by Vulture and his men would turn me toward the nearest convent if I ever got out of here alive.

"Juuuune! Get your sweet little ass out here! My friends are fucking impatient when they're smelling ribs. Got a guy here all the way from Poland, and he could eat a fucking horse – or whatever the fuck they eat in Europe."

I cringed. I couldn't wait in the storage room forever, stacking boxes of booze and sweeping. I came out, wiping my brow, and spied Vulture's group across the main counter in the middle.

"Coming right up!" I yelled, running off to the kitchen before they could bark for anything else.

"Peters, the guys are getting after me about their food…is it ready?" I tensed, eyeing the old cook.

He turned, quickly piling meat that smelled like heaven onto a plate already heavy with fries.

"Here you are, lady," he pushed it into my hands. "I'm working on the next batch. Don't you worry. I know what these guys are like when their bellies are growling and there's nothing but whiskey in 'em."

We exchanged a brief smile. The man worked somewhere else during the day making the best barbecue this side of Montana. By night, the club brought him in for special events, when they had heavy deals on the table unfit for my greasy, haphazard cooking.

"Thanks."

It took both hands to steady the heaping plate of food. I walked it out slowly, carefully moving in the tall black heels they made me wear. The short skirt was riding up my ass, and I twitched in frustration, wishing I could pull it down.

Nothing was worse than showing these dickheads too much. And the 'uniforms' they forced on me and Clara were meant to let everything hang out, to entice them into doing what we feared most.

"Here you go, Mister Vice President. Or is this going to you first, sir?" My eyebrows lifted in surprise.

Ursa, the sixty year old President of this MC was making a rare appearance tonight. It was easy to forget the Missoula charter had a head at all besides Vulture, the VP who ran damned near everything.

President and VP looked at each other. A sly smile appeared on Vulture's face that made me shudder.

Between them sat the Polish guest. He lifted his shot glass, knocked back the amber venom, and smiled right at me.

"Very, very nice, my friends. I think I want to see your show after all," the stranger said in his thick accent.

"Over here, June-o. We're sharing this one." Vulture lifted his hand and wagged me toward him with a finger.

It was tough walking through the narrow space to where he sat. Claws, Scoop, and the rest of the little group certainly didn't push in their chairs to clear more space.

"Here you go," I said, leaning to put the food in front of the VP.

Perfectly positioned. The fist he'd hidden under the table flew out, upending the plate and sending it soaring out of my arms.

I screamed, shocked as ribs and fries rained down around me. Several big meat chunks plopped on my breasts, my shoulders, my calves, smearing me with barbecue.

The men roared with laughter.

I stood in quiet disgust, staring in disbelief as sauce and grease left hot trails on my skin and clothes. The Polish man was laughing so hard he had to blink back tears. The rest of the guys slapped hands, tossing out congratulations on a prank well done.

Now, I understood. I was tonight's entertainment.

No matter how much Clara and I settled here, they'd rudely reminded me the clubhouse would never, ever be home.

"Look at the fucking mess you've created, June bug! Better clean it up."

Everything in my stomach twisted, winding my intestines in hot rage. I wanted to fling the towel I carried in my waitress pouch right at his dirty face.

But I knew my place. I could do what he said, or suffer something a whole lot worse.

Vulture was a greedy, despicable man, but he always backed his word with violence. There were no bluffs.

I moved to the small empty space on the table first, mopping up stray sauce and fries.

When I was done, I pulled away. Vulture grabbed my arm. His fingers dug into my flesh with the same cruel intensity he'd used when they killed Dad and hauled my sister and I here.

"I'm not just talking about this table. *You're* a mess too, bitch. Take off your fucking clothes and clean this shit up. My friends want to see you naked. It'll be good practice before we send you to work at the new pole dancing place next week." His eyes narrowed when he saw my resistance bristling. "Be glad I'm content to give them a show in just your panties – long as you cooperate, darlin'."

Bitter fire boiled in my veins. I burned to scream no, trembled with the need to blow venom in his face. I wanted to bite his fucking nose off and spit it on the table for his friends and brothers to see.

How about that for a show?

I walked away from the table and forced my feet to stop before they got into the hall. I turned, slowly wiggling off my dress, and then undoing my top.

The men shouted and hollered like I was another stripper, another whore who came on the weekends to fuck their nasty brains out. I crawled between their legs, sweeping up the stray food. Up until that moment, I didn't think it could get any worse.

What a fucking idiot I was. Worse wasn't even half of it when greasy fingers grazed my panties, pinching my ass while I cleaned.

The Polish man was the worst.

His breath grew heavy, rugged, full of raging need when he reached between my legs. The sick fuck slipped his finger between my folds once before I jerked away, diving for a rib rolled against Ursa's boot.

"What is it, baby-baby? This little girl is dry as desert! You want I should help, Vulture?"

That's it. You lay your filthy hand on me and I'll bite it. I'll rip away your finger or anything else that comes near my body.

Don't. You. Fucking. Do. It.

"No," Vulture said slowly. "She's doing everything I promised. One thing you'll find about working with this MC is I'm a man of my word. You can look, Jaro, but you don't get to touch her. Go ahead, June bug. Get this shit out of here and go take a hot shower. You've earned it."

I stood, gathering up the last of the fallen food. I blinked in surprise.

Vulture grinned and flashed a wink. His wicked trademark. The Polish man pouted next to him.

I know what Vulture wanted: I was supposed to love him for this, fall to my feet in gratitude for holding back a man who'd love to screw me blind.

Not likely, I thought. *I won't thank you for this. Not for anything.*

I knew the bastard wanted me. Hell, both of us. The crude comments he made about twin sisters were manly jokes around his brothers, but they were also absolute truth.

For some reason I couldn't figure out, he wanted to win me and Clara over, as if we were special prizes. He wanted us as willing, wet, and wild as the groupie whores who came through the clubhouse every weekend, slobbering all over any man with a few patches on his leather jacket.

Quietly fuming, I carried the mess away to the kitchen. A dozen eyes followed my barely clad ass the whole time, making me flush beet red.

Sickness and shame curdled my stomach.

They were still drinking and laughing, carrying on like nothing happened, after I disappeared from view.

Then it hit me.

Why the hell couldn't I see it before? Every night like this was an opportunity, and this one was shaping up to be no different. The club always drank, gorged, and fucked itself into a stupor, unable to move a muscle until morning.

Until morning...I smiled to myself. During the bewitching hours between two and seven a.m., anything might happen.

Anything.

Peters promised to cook up more food and serve it to them by himself. He looked at me sadly when he saw the grease and sauce all over me.

"Rest up, June. I've got the rest of this tonight." He was a kind man, even if he worked for brutal men willingly.

Just make it to the shower like Vulture says. Wait a few hours. When they're passed out and dead to the world, that's when I'll take Clara.

That's when we'll leave this place like we should've done months ago.

The longest night of my life had officially started.

"Clara, come on. We have to go." I shook my sister three times before she groaned and rolled in her bed.

She blinked, eyes big and hazy from the crap she'd smoked earlier. "Huh? Go where? I just wanna go back to bed, June. You...you woke me from a dead sleep."

Gritting my teeth in frustration, I grabbed her arms and pulled her up. I didn't like to hurt her – not when the men had plenty of pain and humiliation for us – but this was an exception.

I slapped her. Hard.

"Ow! What the hell, sis?" Clara held her hot cheek and began to cry.

Damn it, I didn't have time for this.

It was a little past three. Right now, everybody in the club was out, dozing in deep comas.

"We're going to walk right past these fuckers while they're sleeping and go out the front door. They're all asleep. Checked and double checked. We've been here too long, sis...we're losing our will to fight."

Clara rolled her eyes. I seized her shoulders and shook her harder.

"Don't do that! You've got to remember why we're here. Remember the way they killed Dad and probably killed Mom too. Remember."

It wasn't just probably, but I didn't have the heart to tell her I overheard Mom had been found dead weeks ago. Drug overdose.

It didn't surprise me. By now, I was so fucking numb, the news about my mother was just one more insult, one more hazy scene in our waking nightmare.

I shook her. Clara's eyes rolled and she started to weep.

"Why you bringing back shitty memories, June? I've tried so hard to forget. So damned hard! You don't understand." She paused, sucking in a big breath. "I *want* to forget, June. I want to lose myself in work and sleep and smoking…I want to erase everything and start all over."

Her lip quivered. My heart swelled with sympathy, even through my annoyance.

My sister hadn't held up as well as I. It was like something broke when we arrived at the clubhouse. She lived like a fucking zombie, rarely showing any emotion except fits of crying which shook her whole body.

She lived pretty straight while we were growing up. Now, she tried to get blazed on garbage every night, whatever she could scavenge from the clubhouse's medicine cabinet or underhanded Prospects.

I was the only one who kept the will to fight burning, and not very well. Clara had her heart torn to shreds at once. Mine was coming undone slowly, blow by savage blow.

Each day we spent in this hellhole meant surrendering another small piece of myself, accepting this dungeon as home.

We needed to get out, and we had to do it now.

Holding Clara's head, I looked at her, trying to reach her through the tears and shaking.

Christ. If we really get out of here, she's gonna need a shrink. Dunno how we'll afford the pros to get her head straight.

"I just need you to listen, okay? Follow me. Every step I take, you mirror it. Stay quiet and stick close behind me. We'll be out of here before you know it. You can *really* start over then, Clara. We'll be free."

I almost started crying when I spoke the last word. Good thing I didn't, especially when my sis was finally settling down.

"Free to go *where?*" Clara's eyes were huge, like a puppy looking for a question its master had no way to answer.

I bit my lip. I didn't have a fucking clue, but right now, *anywhere* was going to be better than the Grizzlies MC Missoula clubhouse.

"Come on. Stay behind me and keep quiet."

Clara had lost a lot of weight since we arrived. Her wrist was skinny and frail when I pulled her along, into the hallway leading through the bar.

If we could just tiptoe past the fuckers slumped in their chairs or passed out half naked on the floor…

In the beginning, all seemed well. There weren't too many guys laying around to trip over.

We only stepped over two, maybe three, bloated bodies.

I took extra care not to get my heel caught on their sprawling leather jackets. Clara followed, a little more shakily, but she did it.

Going through the door wouldn't be easy. The buzzer would sound. With any luck, they'd think it was just someone stepping out for a smoke, or maybe to barf up ribs and whiskey and God knows what else they'd sucked down their gullets.

Almost there…almost!

"Hey, June! Look!" Clara's wrist slipped from my hand.

She stood next to the wall and giggled. I looked back. By some terrible coincidence, my poor, dumb sister just happened to see the old black and white photo of Dad on his bike.

Beneath the dust covering the photo, he stood by his Harley smiling, holding two baby girls in his arms. Mom leaned over his shoulder, a thousand times prettier than the last time we saw her. No junkie blemishes circled her eyes or stained her skin.

Some asshole had written RAT over Dad's chest in black marker. I was surprised they'd let it go at that and hadn't scrubbed his image from existence.

My heart throbbed. Clara's face crinkled. The air went out her lungs and panic set in. Horrified, I knew what was about to happen, and I couldn't stop it.

She was one breath away from crying. Once she started sobbing all over the place, our chances were ruined.

"Fucking come on, sis! We can look at photos later...come on!"

I pulled at her. Hard. Clara wasn't budging.

"Fucking stop it, June! Let me look. Just another minute. Please! I've forgotten what he looked like..."

Near the bar, a man smacked his lips and grunted. My eyes snapped over to him and made sure he wasn't getting up.

All clear. By some miracle, he rolled and slumped on his face.

"Clara!" I hissed. "Let's go. We're almost there."

"No, no, no," she bawled, staring past me at the darkness outside. "There's nothing out there for us. Everything we had died right here!"

She jammed her pointer finger hard into the picture and cracked the glass. I looked up, trying to decide how best to drag my own sister out of this place without her kicking and screaming.

Then the door behind me swung open, and all my worries about escape evaporated. Vulture stood there, wiping his head and slicking back his long hair. He didn't see us at first while his eyes adjusted to the dim light, and his hangover probably bought us two more seconds.

Not nearly enough.

"Hey, what the fuck? What the hell are you two doing out here?" The realization hit him and I saw *the look*.

He didn't look playful in the cruel way he usually did when he toyed with us. The cold eyed killer was back, the same expression he'd worn when he admired my Dad's body like a sculpture he'd molded in his own bony hands.

"Are you fucking bitches goin' where I think you're goin'?"

I swallowed hard. Vulture took another step forward, breathing hot and angry through his mouth. Cheap tobacco turned his breath into a hot, reeking wind.

"Ungrateful little cunts!" Vulture lunged, tearing at my hair.

Pain blinded me. I thought he'd tear my hair out, but he must've been too distracted by grabbing Clara in the other hand.

We buckled halfway to the ground and struggled to keep up as he dragged us down the hallway, back toward our rooms.

When I saw the door to our freedom disappearing, I screamed. He twisted my hair that much harder, digging his dirty fingers into my earlobe for extra pain.

"Huh?" One guy on the ground we'd stepped over in the hall wiped his eyes.

"Wake the fuck up!" Vulture kicked him in the side. "Come with me, Scoop. Caught these little whores trying to get away without paying their dues."

"Jesus!" Scoop bolted to his feet, shaking off his coma.

"The worst part is I tried," he said darkly.

"I tried to give you girls a home. I tried to be fucking nice. But obviously I'm a fucking retard for thinking you two ungrateful shits would see it!" He kicked in the door to our room.

It hit the wall, and we screamed as he threw us inside. I landed on the floor so hard my ribs shook. Clara spun, curled herself into a ball, and began to blubber.

She looked so much like Mom the last time we'd seen her, before they shot her up with heroine and stole her from us forever. Crazy sadness flickered in her eyes, but defeat overwhelmed everything else.

We were beaten. Now, the victors were going to make us pay.

I rolled, holding my ribs. Two dark shadows stood over us. I closed my eyes.

It was hell trying to shut my brain down as my heart beat wild in my chest. What I'd feared most was imminent, if they didn't just decide to slit our throats on the spot.

Vulture planted his big hands on his knees and leaned down, until his eyes matched my level.

"Now, you listen up June-o, because I know you're the ring leader here. I could beat your little ass raw and drive my cock up it 'til you need a plastic bag to shit through." He paused. "But I'm not going to do that."

His breath smelled like rancid ashes. I coughed, forced my eyes open, and looked into the dark gems set in his head.

Hellfire blazed there. Pure evil.

"What's stopping you? You want to punish me...I don't care anymore.." The words barely squeaked out of my throat.

He's right about one thing: this is my doing. I'm ready to accept the consequences, no matter how horrific.

"Brave little June bug." With a heavy sigh, Vulture shot up, threw his head back, and laughed. "Sometimes I wish you were a man. You would've made a better addition to this MC than your shitty old daddy. You're a hard one to break. Lucky for both of us, I like hard."

He lifted one hand and snapped his fingers. "Scoop! You start in on the little cunt mewling like a kitten over there. I'll make sure this one doesn't do anything stupid while you get her pussy warmed up for me."

Clara screamed as soon as the biker's grimy hands were on her. Scoop forced her to the floor and pushed down her jeans, pinching her bare thighs as he ran his hands up the middle.

"Clara! Jesus Christ. You can't do this!" I shouted. "Please, Vulture. I'm begging you! No, no, no...no."

My sister howled again. The beast between her legs grabbed her panties and ripped them down in one jerk. His filthy fingers moved deeper, into places they never should've been. A mean erection bulged in his pants between them, ready to replace his fingers anytime.

"No!" I jerked forward. I couldn't let this happen!

My sweet, broken, beautiful sister shouldn't pay for my mistake in a world that had any justice.

Running into Vulture was like colliding with a brick wall. He grabbed my wrists to steady me, giving me a good jerk.

Every fiber of my being shot hatred into his eyes. No, escape wasn't an option anymore. I had to murder this asshole, anything to make sure he stopped hurting everyone I loved.

He forced my legs apart and rammed his hips into mine, making me feel the sick hardness he had between his legs.

"Sit back down and shut up, cunt. Be happy you're not in her place. I'm gonna tear her virgin hole apart and lick the blood up later. Show a little fucking gratitude for once in your miserable life. You don't have to feel this ripping you open like her," he banged his hips on mine again. "Not tonight, anyway."

Clara screamed. My eyes glanced over Vulture's shoulder, and ice cold pain shot up my back. Scoop had one hand on his open fly, fishing out his erection. The other hand held Clara brutally by the chin, jerking her toward the split in his pants.

"Bastard!" I spat in his face. "God. Damn. You."

Vulture reached up and wiped my spittle off his cheek. His eyes flashed with angry malevolence.

"Stupid bitch!"

The back of his hand slammed into my cheek so hard the whole room turned red, drowned in a curtain of blood. I topped to the floor, hit my head, and everything turned black.

When I woke up, everything was deathly still. My brain hummed something fierce.

I saw the crumpled heap laying on the cot across the room.

Clara!

I ran over. She lay very still. Something was clutched tight in her small hands.

"Clara? Sis?" I shook her.

My heart stopped when I realized she wasn't breathing at all. Her skin was unnaturally cold. Pale. Dead.

"Oh, God!" I crumpled to my knees and hugged her close, pulling her toward me as I fell. "God!"

Her arms flopped aside and packets of pills spilled out around her breasts. I saw the cartons were torn and empty.

Trembling, I reached out and picked up a half-shredded box. Sleeping pills, the same shit she'd been hording to stop the bad dreams at night.

I knew she had them, but I never, ever thought they'd be used like this.

Her bare thighs were streaked with blood. They killed her – murdered my precious sister – even if she'd taken matters into her own hands as soon as they tossed her aside like a used condom.

My heart dropped into my legs and never came up. The last shred of dignity and hope I had died right along with her.

When Vulture came up behind me later that morning, admiring his work, I didn't even look up. There was no sense in fighting anymore.

The need for vengeance was as sharp and distant as the angry spasms in my stomach. But I couldn't feed it now. I couldn't do anything but whimper like a beaten puppy when he ran his horrible fingers through my hair.

"Dead?" he asked, sounding a little surprised. "Never saw that one coming. Guess the little bitch had more guts than I gave her credit for."

I didn't answer. His nasty fingers pinched my shoulder, the same way he grabbed me when I saw Dad dead in the sink.

"I'm glad this happened, June bug. I only meant to hurt her and teach her lesson. Maybe it's better this way," he said coldly. "She's not our problem anymore. You're free to focus on yourself, and I think we have a special understanding here. Even a dumb bitch like you gets it, doesn't she?"

Now he pinched my chin, forcing me to lean and look at him. I almost vomited all over his jeans and cut, the leather jacket bearing the monstrous symbols that destroyed my life.

The word PRESIDENT filled my eyes. It may as well have said LUCIFER.

"Answer me. I won't ask a second time. Sick of fucking repeating myself with you girls."

"Yes." My voice was quiet. Detached. "We have an understanding."

Vulture gave me the biggest smile in the world, leaving the cruelty in his eyes. The painful pinch stopped. He moved his hand away and clapped me on the shoulder like he did with his brothers.

"I'm real happy to hear that. You start at the Dirty Diamond next week. Keep your head down. Do your fucking work like a good girl. I'll make sure you don't end up like your sister. Even give her a nice send off for you and make sure her ashes make their way to your parent's plot. We good?"

He squeezed my shoulder again. I didn't shake outwardly, but everything inside me was spinning, lost and wild in an infinite void of blackness.

"Yeah. We're good."

For two years, I danced. I learned to take the catcalls, the jeers, to climb up on the stage and shake my tits and ass.

I wasn't another heap of pretty meat on stage. I was the best damned dancer, the favorite, probably because everybody thought my numbness was an act. Like playing hard to get.

The Dirty Diamond's clients were mostly average joes with a taste for loose women. They loved the way the way I never offered more than a lap dance. Every man wanted to be the one to get behind the dark mystery in my eyes.

I overheard their whispers, and I didn't care.

A tiny part of me enjoyed their easy-to-please presence. Every minute at the Dirty Diamond meant one more away from the Grizzlies clubhouse, where Vulture and his pigs reigned.

Incredibly, the devil kept his word. Not long after Clara's urn was buried in a cheap plot next to Mom and Dad, new whores moved in, new girls with perfect skin and sharp tongues offered up by the Polish man.

I stayed out of their way, and they were happy to return the favor.

They were hotter than me and willing to worship cocks at the MC. Vulture and the boys had new love interests. They started fucking left and right, and a couple of the better guys claimed old ladies.

Whatever the deal with the Polish man involved, it had brought them drugs and women. Lots and lots of both. Harder shit moved in.

Tweaking on coke and other crap got so bad during the winter Vulture had to lay down the law so his guys could still ride their bikes without wrecking them.

I receded into the background, forgotten in my room when I returned there to sleep.

All they cared about was the money I brought in by becoming the new strip joint's number one mover and shaker.

Time passed in a haze. Days yawned into weeks, and then weeks blurred into months.

Two more years went by in a hollow blink. I was nearly old enough to drink the night my soul returned, suddenly unchained from its depths.

The strangers did it. As soon as they came swaggering into the Dirty Diamond, I knew something was seriously different.

They were men with leather jackets and the same gruff, dangerous aura every outlaw carried who wore the 1% patch. But they weren't Grizzlies.

I was up on the stage. I'd just gotten started when they came in and took up a table near the front.

I was so into the routine I'd worked a thousand times I didn't notice him at first, just his group, the mysterious intruders.

When I finally saw him, the whole world seemed to stop. I almost lost my footing as I swung around the pole, popping my ass toward the crowd, trying to clear my head and forget my miserable life.

The big man in the middle of the table was watching me.

His eyes flickered with masculine heat, a gaze a million times more intense than the ones that drooled over me day and night.

His eyes said *I want you,* but it wasn't just my flesh he was after. His hard gaze demanded everything – body, mind, and soul.

He was tall, powerful, probably in his early thirties. Clean cut compared to the Grizzlies. Some prickly stubble lined his cheeks, but he was missing the tangled beard and grease they wore like bad cologne.

His face was hard. It wasn't evil. His curious intensity only grew as I peeled off my panties and thrust my body at the leering men circling the stage.

This man never licked his lips or patted his crotch. He never jeered or reached into his wallet and walked crumpled dollars up to the stage.

He just sat tall and watched like I was something incredible, even while his buddies whispered and ribbed him with their elbows over beers.

Total presence. Watching him was like watching a time bomb waiting to go off.

And go off, he did, as soon as the Grizzlies came in.

It was Claws and that asshole Scoop, prowling at the stage's edges to leer at me. They always did while I was working, a sickly reminder that I was never completely free, even when I wasn't at the clubhouse.

Scoop always took keen interest because I looked just like her, Clara, the woman he'd helped murder with his lust. If I ever fucked up, Vulture wouldn't hesitate to sic him on me like a hungry dog.

I never got the chance to stop and worry about what Scoop would do. The man with the intense eyes got up, walked over to where he was standing, and threw him to the floor.

Claws instantly began punching his back. The other strangers threw themselves into the brawl, turning over tables and shouting. Patrons ran for the door.

I grabbed my underwear off the floor and went running for the corner. I dressed and crouched on the floor as a beer bottle came sailing onto the stage, shattering into smithereens.

I didn't dare move backstage with shit flying. Had to stay low on the floor in case somebody started shooting.

The chaos stopped. I blinked, looked up, and saw all the overturned tables and broken glass on the floor. The Dirty Diamond had truly become dirty as hell.

Claws was knocked out flat on the floor. The big man who'd watched me held Scoop by his cut, pressing him flat against the stage.

"Last chance, asshole. I'll burn this place to the fucking ground if you want to keep this fight going," the stranger said.

"Okay, dammit! I'm not authorized to do shit without Vulture's approval. Lemme call my VP."

Grudgingly, the man let Scoop get on his feet. The Grizzlies enforcer paced the floor, nursing a bloody nose. I couldn't hear what he was saying.

Nobody had ever drawn blood from him. He won all the fights that broke out in the clubhouse over silly shit. Watching the bright red trickle harden to caked brown beneath his nose made me smile.

"It's done. You've made your point, dickhead." Scoop spat the last word in a hurry, as if he was afraid to say it. "VP says we've got an understanding. We'll let you assholes fuck around in Python, seeing how it's not formally our territory. But you ever come to Missoula again and trash one our businesses, every charter ten states over *will* kick your brains out your asses."

"Good." The stranger grinned. "I like to fight fair. Now get the fuck out of my way and let me take my collateral."

"Collateral?" Scoop spread his legs like he was ready to go for a re-match.

"Yeah, asshole. You said your VP brokered a deal. I'm gonna assume things work here out West the same as they do with every other MC from here to Maine. Collateral means we won't torch this place to the ground, and you boys'll have extra incentive to keep your word."

Scoop chewed his bloody lip, repressing a volcanic anger. A big guy with the stranger pushed him aside, and my jaw dropped a little when he didn't shove back.

Blood rushed into my ears, hot and steamy and scared. Bright eyes was heading right for me.

I hadn't felt true paralyzing terror since the night they killed Clara. But he brought it back, shot such blinding intensity into my brain I nearly passed out before he was at my side, a godly silhouette above me, reaching out.

"What is it?" I moaned. "What the hell do you want?"

"Get up, babe. I'm Maverick, President of the Prairie Devils MC, and I'm here to get you out of this shithole."

II: Gold Rush on Wheels
(Maverick)

I've always said there's nothing in this world like the roar of the open road and the wind in my face, even when it's colder than a witch's tit.

"You feel that frost in your beard yet?" I said over the radio clipped to my helmet. "Don't tell me I'm gonna have to thaw you boys out over the fire when we get to grandpa's house."

"I can still feel my fucking face, so there's that." My half-brother, Blaze, rode right behind me. "Let's keep up the pace, Maverick. Would be nice to get there before sundown when Jack Frost really starts blowing something fierce."

I smiled, watching him wipe the ice cold skin on his chin behind his visor. Hypno and Shatter trailed him, all four of us who made up our small Nomad charter.

It was a long drive from central Minnesota where my boys and I had stayed the winter, taking care of business for our founding charter in North Dakota. Now, we were almost back in Cassandra, a dusty little town just West of Fargo, birthplace of the Prairie Devils Motorcycle Club.

I'd been a Nomad for nearly ten years since I patched into the club, and President of this charter for three.

Best part about being a Nomad? We didn't answer to fucking anybody.

Nobody except Throttle, President of the mother charter, who'd called us home on business.

Hell, it wasn't even right to call the Cassandra clubhouse grandpa's house anymore. Throttle's old man, Voodoo, the guy who started the whole club back in Nixon's day, was killed last year during our war with the Raging Skulls.

Since then, his son had taken over. He ran a pretty tight ship from what I'd heard, despite a few growing pains.

New boss. Better be the same as the old boss for our purposes.

I swallowed, gulping down Springtime air, cold and fresh. The plains were half-frozen, caked with snow reflecting silver and orange.

Pretty damned weird to visit mother charter so early in the year this far north.

When mother charter called, everybody was willing to help. It seemed like we were the only ones who weren't there for the big dust up with the Raging Skulls MC last year. They took out Voodoo, hit Cassandra hard, and nearly took down Throttle too before he put them in their place.

I doubted he needed us for anything too serious. Nothing as bad as another war between clubs with the recent drama behind them.

Good fucking riddance.

Still, I wondered…what the hell were we going to find there? The man wasn't calling us home for whiskey floats like some kinda ice cream social.

Being a Nomad means being free. In this charter, a man has the same privileges as the rest of the Prairie Devils brotherhood, but without the politics and the bullshit that goes on in the clubs with one place they call home.

And God willing, I was gonna keep it that way.

My brothers hit the bar to warm up with whiskey and burgers as soon as we were inside. I marched straight back to the office attached to the meeting room.

The door was half-cracked. A huge Prairie Devils MC emblem hung on the door, the devil's face surrounded by pitchforks. Same as the patches on our jackets, except blown up in a way that made anybody wearing these colors want to give it a sharp salute.

I raised my fist above the emblem and knocked.

"Come on in!"

I walked through, shut the door behind me, and stared as Throttle rose. He smiled and stepped through the cramped space separating his desk from the wall.

"It's been a long time, brother!" Throttle embraced me, pounding my back.

He was a little younger than me, but he had Voodoo's edge. Not to mention his old man's spitting image too.

I slapped him on the back one more time and he let me go. Throttle fumbled with bottom drawer to the huge filing cabinet behind him. I smiled when I saw it was filled with something way more interesting than manila folders.

He pulled out a fresh bottle of Jack and set down two tumblers. My stomach growled, hungry to feel its sweet, comforting burn even more than I wanted some grub.

"Well, chief, what brings us here?" I took my glass and took a long sip.

Heat exploded in my guts. Pure heaven after a six hour ride through a late Midwestern winter.

"You're a spirited man, aren't you, brother? Always ready to go." Throttle cocked his head, eyeing me closely. "My VP, Warlock, says I almost had to call you up myself to keep you in Minnesota last summer."

I laughed. "Yeah. I like to keep my fists fresh when the club's in trouble. You know me. I love a good fight when it's for a good cause."

I folded my fingers and cracked my knuckles. Cassandra's President nodded.

"That's what I thought, and it's the reason you're here." He picked up his glass, swirling around the amber liquid at the bottom. "Now that we've got our heads straight after breaking up the Skulls, it's time to take on new opportunities and get some fucking money flowing. I want you to head West, Maverick. There's a little town called Python just south of Missoula. Perfect place to set up another charter and bring this MC to the wild West."

I gulped the other half of my whiskey and clinked the class on the table.

"Montana," I repeated. "Isn't that Grizzlies territory?"

"Just a sliver now. I've done my homework and the Grizzlies MC is stretched pretty thin these days. Their club doesn't even do much in Bozeman and Billings anymore. They pissed off a lot of people when we fought them outside Sturgis a few years ago."

"Who could forget?" I smiled, tasting whiskey on my lips.

I'd personally clobbered at least four big guys during that dust up. The Grizzlies were strong, but we beat them then, and Throttle smelled blood.

"I told you, I crunched the numbers. If we get ourselves a charter out there, we've got a pipeline straight up to Alberta. Maybe Idaho too if they're weaker than I think. Two point seven million dollars to start. Chew on that for a minute." He raised his fist and extended his pointer finger at me.

"That's a lot of fucking bills, brother."

"Damned straight. And that's just for the first few shipments up to our friends north of the border. The Grizzlies never got up to Vancouver and Calgary. Hell, they've been struggling to hold down Boise with all the shit going on with their southern flank. The Mexican cartels are muscling in on their turf. Tearing them a new asshole out in California."

"And that's where I come in," I finished. It didn't take a psychic to know where this was heading.

Throttle flashed me his trademark grin. "Exactly. Look, I know playing custodian isn't your style."

I nodded. Throttle's face went serious, sizing me up.

"I need you on this. I know you like a good fight, even though I'm really asking you to play pioneer. We can't go head to head with the Grizzlies unless they make us. But if they decide to break into our new shop while we're setting it up, then there's no man I'd rather have at the tip of the spear."

The compliment was genuine. Wasn't just blowing smoke up my ass.

Honest Jack. That's what some guys had taken to calling him behind his back, a play on his real name instead of his MC handle. *Can't say no to confidence like that in these bones.*

Not that I had much choice turning down a direct order from the mother charter. When mom called his kids, we all answered, and were fucking glad to do it.

I extended my hand. "You've got yourself a deal, brother. Just as long as you let me get back to what I do best after everything's rocking in the mountains."

He grinned and shook my hand, edging his fingers up to my wrists. He eyed the place where the club's pitchfork symbol began, inks I'd gotten tattooed on these guns years ago.

"I wouldn't ask a Nomad to settle down forever. Until then, we're gonna send your cut to Frannie so she can spruce up those patches. Congrats. You're the new President of the Prairie Devils Python charter."

Throttle and I carried on our conversation in the famous bar. He was telling me all about how his charter had mopped the floor with the town's corrupt mayor last year, the asshole who'd set up the brutal war with the Skulls.

I was feeling good. Tight lightning buzzed in my stomach from my fourth shot of Jack.

"Fuck, brother, where are those burgers? I'm gonna be running on pure fumes here if they don't show up soon."

As if on cue, two women walked out carrying heaping platters of cheeseburgers and fries. It was Frannie, the charter's oldest and wisest old lady. She belonged to the VP, Warlock.

Also had a younger girl at her side I didn't recognize, until she flashed her teeth at Throttle.

"Here you go, boys," she said sweetly.

"What the fuck, baby girl?" Throttle's eyebrows shot up. "You're like a month out from delivering our baby and you're carrying piles of steaming food over our kid?"

"Oh, give the girl some credit, Jack." Frannie pushed my plate in front of me and clapped her President on the shoulder. "She's been doing just fine. I cut her hours patching up your boys, just like you asked."

"Yeah, Jack. Frannie's right. She always is. You know I wouldn't do anything to screw with our kid." She threw her arms around his neck and ran her fingers through his hair. "There's nothing I keep closer to my heart, love, except maybe you."

Damn, they were tight. Only two ladies around who could get away with calling him by anything but his road name.

"And that's why I love you, Rach." Growling, Throttle wrapped his arm around her waist and pulled her close.

How the hell did I forget? This was Rachel, the girl who'd been caught in the crossfire during the war with the Skulls. Her fuckhead father was the town's Mayor the club now had under heavy guard, dangling his puppet strings for our benefit.

Fucker deserved it too. He tried to rip Rach away from Throttle and sell her into slavery.

"Good to meet you. The grub smells delicious, ladies," I said.

No lie. I was seriously enthusiastic. I smashed the burger in my fingers and lifted it to my lips. I was about to sink my teeth into that juicy thing when there was an explosive crash.

Two guys went down on the other side of the bar. They were yelling, throwing punches, screaming at the top of their lungs.

"Fucking shit! Better not be one of my guys." I threw my burger down on the plate, annoyed as all hell.

Throttle jumped out of Rachel's embrace. We shared a second of mutual frustration and went running toward the commotion.

My boys and the Cassandra guys were all gathered in a circle, laughing and throwing insults like a bunch of school boys watching their first fight. Relief steamed out my lungs when I saw the two fighters weren't part of my crew.

There was a huge guy on top of a skinny, wiry man covered in tattoos. The big guy looked like a giant stuffed into clothes one size too small.

Some petty shit had probably started the fight, but his fists were gonna do serious damage to the scrawny guy if they landed on his head.

I jumped in right behind Throttle, tugging on the giant's fists with both hands. Goliath roared in frustration as the skinny dude rolled out of harm's way. He swung his fists, hurling me backward.

Fuck, I rolled hard, out of control, bowling over several Cassandra brothers and almost plowing into Throttle's old lady too. I stood up fast, shooting Rach an apologetic smile.

"What the fuck?" I turned around to face the scene.

The skinny guy was flattened against the wall smiling. Throttle stood over the big guy, who was on his knees. Muscles bulged in his huge neck like a cartoon.

"Freak here started, it, boss! Told me he was gonna do the nasty with my girl. You can't expect me to lay down and let him shit all over me!" He slapped his huge fists on his knees.

"Your girl? That's not what Julie told me last night, brother," the thin guy called Freak said. "Said she was just getting to know everybody here while she was riding my cock. You're not her old man and you're a fucking idiot to throw punches over a club whore."

The big guy stood, snorting and ready to charge. He literally looked like a fucking bull. I moved in, just in case Throttle needed backup. I watched our fearless leader shake his head.

Then Throttle's hands shot out like shields and hit the big guy in the chest. He grabbed his jacket, stretching it up around his head.

"Tank, you stupid, stupid motherfucker. Did all the time overseas knock something loose in your skull? Well?" Throttle's voice exploded, and he shook the giant's collar.

"Sorry, boss. I was just – "

"Picking fights over a new whore who isn't yours! You realize you almost knocked another President right into my pregnant old lady?" Throttle pointed, screaming in his face.

"I…I'm sorry, boss. Really. I got carried away."

Without another word, Throttle kneed him in the stomach. The giant winced, and then rocked back as his President's fist connected with his jaw.

"That's for fucking endangering people on my watch over a bunch of bullshit. If you didn't help us out so much with the Skulls, I'd be taking out my knife and cutting off your patches right now."

A few guys snickered next to me. Throttle spun, shooting them with an icy gaze that froze the laughs.

"Shit's not funny, brothers. These are the times when being MC Prez really sucks bull cock."

Alarm showed in Tank's eyes. I'd never seen a man so big and muscular so fucking afraid. The whole weird scene almost made me forget my nagging hunger for my lonely burger.

"I'm gonna give you one more chance, asshole. Maverick!" Throttle called my name. "Take this sorry son of a bitch with you tomorrow and see if you can make a man out of him. I'm counting on you to do what the US Army couldn't with this impulsive fuck."

Tank looked at me like a lost dog and I pinched my teeth together.

Fucking-A. Setting up shop in Grizzlies territory just got fucking harder.

"Godspeed, boys. I'm not the only one counting on you to pull this shit off. You're carrying the whole MC's reputation on your backs now." Throttle extended his hand.

I shook it, sucking in the cool morning air. My boys and I were on our bikes, ready to blow Cassandra for the fifteen hour drive to Python, Montana.

"Won't let you down," I said sincerely.

"I know. And if Tank or anybody else gives you trouble out there, you know my number. I'll come over myself and kick their asses into line."

I narrowed my eyes. What the fuck? Throttle knew damned well I was capable of handling my own men.

He turned and stepped away. In my mirror, I saw him heading toward the small pregnant girl on the steps leading into the club.

When he got to her, he picked her up and gave her the biggest bear hug I'd ever seen. They twisted together in the new dawn light, lovely-dovey to the extreme.

My irritation softened. Claiming an old lady had changed him. Mostly for the better.

He wasn't giving me needless assurances just to wave his dick. The man was really confident, on top of the fucking world.

Throttle the family man was alien to everything I knew, but it made me smile.

"Come on, boys," I said, switching on my radio and revving my engine. "Let's get this long fucking ride over with. New guy, you stick close behind Shatter and Hypno. We're not gonna treat you like a prospect again, but you better learn fast how shit works in the Nomads."

"You're the boss," Tank said over the line.

We took off, with Blaze several feet back and the rest of my boys behind me. It had been awhile since I rode fifteen hours over the open prairie, into the rugged terrain out West.

The MC rarely took the chance to cut through enemy territory. The Grizzlies presence in big sky country had been like a fucking iron curtain for at least the past decades, keeping us landlocked in the Midwest.

At the third fill-up stop in Bozeman, the new guy hopped off his bike and stretched. I took a good look at what a big gorilla he really was.

Tank, huh? Good name for him. If only I could make his fists work for me in this well oiled machine I called my charter.

We rode on.

It was dark and my bones were chattering something fierce when we finally got into Python. Good thing the little mountain valleys didn't have the same wicked winds as the open plains we'd left behind.

"Jes-ussss," Blaze whistled when we rolled up to the old building. "You telling me this is the place? I heard it was an old topless bar – but fuck! Looks more like a saloon that hasn't seen any good days since Jesse James."

"Welcome home, brother." I gave him a good crack on the back. "This is our clubhouse to set up and tweak to our liking until Throttle doesn't need us here anymore."

Behind us, the other guys tried to stifle their laughter. I turned, a wry grin on my face.

"Don't laugh your guts up too hard, boys. This rat's nest is where we're all staying until the bear gives us some room." I reached into my pocket and fished out the key to the front door. "Let's go. We've got a lot of work to do."

A lot of work? Yeah, one hell of an understatement.

It took more than a week to make the place habitable. We didn't even get a fully stocked bar until our third night there, when Tank helped unload some kind donations from locals who were curious about our MC.

"Supporters already? Shit, brother. That's a new record," Blaze said, puffing on a cigarette.

We were taking a break after directing the movers to bring in our new furniture. Finally, the end was in sight. A coat of paint for the walls, a few neon lights, Prairie Devils MC flags, and we'd be in business.

"We're gonna need 'em. This is deadly close to enemy territory. I'm not gonna turn down having some folks on our side in this little town."

One of the movers carrying in snacks and drinks stopped. He looked at me nervously, blinking his eyes. The new President patch I wore with PRAIRIE DEVILS MC, PYTHON stitched under it had caught his eye.

"What's the matter? Don't tell me you've never seen an MC's colors before?"

"No, it's not that," he held his hands out. "Some of us are just damned glad to see you guys."

What the hell? That's the first I've heard any ordinary folks being happy to see a pack of strange one-percenters rolling into town.

"Why's that?" I had to ask. The stranger piqued my curiosity.

"Anybody's better than the Grizzlies." He made a sour face. "Those fucks have been dragging their dirt through Python since I was a old enough to pop wood at a pretty girl. Sheriff won't do shit because they snagged the local cops in a brutality case a few years back. Killed a few more to seal the deal."

I nodded. The Grizzlies were conniving bastards.

They used their big numbers to intimidate, and ambushes were their favorite. It took the Devils plus several allied groups to chase them off Sturgis.

"Look, I know you guys aren't saints," the man said. "But I think you're better for this town than they are."

Smiling, I fingered the 1% patch beneath President, and then turned around and showed him my top rocker. "You're right about that. The details are in the name."

"Devils. I get it. You're outlaws," he said. "Frankly, I don't give a shit. If you run off the Grizzlies without terrorizing folks who're just trying to go about their business, we'll look the other way when you guys make your money. I volunteered to lend some support because I want them gone for good, and so does everybody else in this town."

The man went back to work. Blaze turned to me, stroking his short beard.

"That's one hell of an offer. Maybe getting ourselves a fort out here won't be so bad after all."

"Think again, brother. It's gonna be a knock down, drag out fucking fight. The Grizzlies won't give up easy, even if all four hundred people in this town are standing behind us. We're gonna have to fight for what we want, and hold onto everything we take."

The clubhouse was finished, or close enough to it. My guys were getting restless, tired of painting walls and moving furniture.

It was time to take a trial run and see what the hell we were dealing with in the great unknown.

That night, we rolled north of Python, into Grizzlies territory proper. The man I'd talked to in the new clubhouse pointed me to the rival MC's nearest operation.

It was a little strip club just outside Missoula called the Dirty Diamond. The five of us parked our bikes along the main drag and stretched. I watched a couple guys pat their pockets, checking on the weapons we'd readied before we hit the road.

I hoped to hell we wouldn't have to shake anything bigger and deadlier than our fists. But the Grizzlies' response, if any, was gonna determine what happened tonight.

We were here to deliver a message, and nothing was gonna stop us.

I was the first one in. The place was low lit, smoky, and crowded. No different than any other strip joint I'd been to.

The locals must've thought we were Grizzlies. We were the only ones wearing leather, and a path to a table near the stage automatically opened for us.

I wasn't used to being treated like royalty for wearing the patch. But it was weird to see the sheer terror in guy's faces as they jerked back and kept their distance.

Terror, not unease.

My brothers pulled up chairs. We sat, ordered a couple beers, and scoped the place out.

Damn it. Where the fuck are our new friends? Not even one guy to watch over their property?

I stiffened. I'd been ready for a fight the minute we stepped through the doors. Not having one made me way more anxious than staring down ten mean looking Grizzlies.

A waitress came around with our beers and I looked toward the stage for the first time.

The girl up there swinging around the pole was bathed in the same burgundy light as the rest of us. She danced well, thrusting up and down the metal stake with her full length, shaking her tits and hair in perfect sync.

And fuck, those were some amazing tits. The girl was full bodied in a way that surprised me.

Most joints like this only trotted out the skinny girls, especially the ones with softball sized implants. I'd always liked a little meat on a woman's bones, and this girl had plenty in *all* the right places.

All natural too. Fucking perfect hourglass.

"I don't see anybody here, Prez," Shatter leaned over and whispered to me. "You think the dude was wrong about this being a Grizzlies hole?"

"No." I pointed toward their emblem on the side door.

The guys looked around nervously. I should've been on alert too, pretending to sip my beer and waiting to kick some ass.

But instead, this fucking beauty stole my attention, anchoring my eyes to her flesh like I hadn't seen a woman for a solid year.

My cock twitched in my jeans. I shifted, opening my legs, anything to relieve the pressure.

There was something about her. She wasn't flashing her pearly whites and blowing kisses like most girls. The odd hoots and hollers from the locals went straight over her head. She didn't acknowledge a single one of them, as if she didn't give a rat's ass about tips at all.

She just danced, wearing the same cold pout the entire time. A few minutes in, her eyes met mine across the dingy lounge. I sat up a little taller, and felt something downright electric shoot through my veins.

Fuck. Was a little more energy brightening her eyes too?

What's going on here? She's a nice strong cocktail on two sexy legs and one fine ass. Spilling emotion out those sad pretty eyes like nothing I've ever seen.

Keep looking this way, baby. See the need in these eyes?

It's not limp desire. It's a fucking promise that I'm gonna see a whole lot more of you soon.

Up close, personal, and wetter than you've been in your life.

"Boss…" I didn't even look over as Tank tried to get my attention. "There's a couple mean looking SOBs with cuts walking down the left side."

"Over there!" Blaze hissed in my ear.

Shit. I didn't want to take my eyes off her, but duty called.

They weren't bullshitting. The Grizzlies had arrived, two big bastards with mean looking jackets. They hadn't seen us.

My hands automatically curled into fists as I watched them from the side. They were looking at the lady up there like she was a piece of fucking meat they'd had before. Jealousy churned in my stomach, and then a nasty need to take her away from them.

Takes a special kinda girl to make me jealous. Special didn't begin to describe the wild, hot, and very jealous need to hammer those fucks into the ground as they ogled her.

She wasn't giving them a single glance, and the girl had to know they were there, right under her. If they'd had her, the feelings weren't mutual.

Just thinking about it made my fists fucking hungry. I stood, shoving my chair against another table.

"Prez? You okay?" Hypno got to his feet before the words were out of his mouth, and so did the other three.

"Just follow my lead," I said.

Instinct took over. The biggest guy filled my killer eyes, the man I meant to take down first. For once, we'd gotten the jump on the Grizzlies with raw numbers.

Not that it would've held me back. The way this fuck practically drooled through his shitty grin made me want to send his teeth flying through the Dirty Diamond like rice at a wedding.

"Hey, asshole."

I tapped him on the shoulder once. He turned, eyes glazed in a stupor.

He hadn't even processed the insult before my knuckles slammed into his jaw. He bleated like a big animal going down, and I swung again, kicking him to the floor while his buddy went at me.

I just love a good bear hunt, I thought with giddy rage ripping through my body.

I ignore the three blows he landed on my back. Too busy pounding the other guy to pieces.

My guys were right in the nick of time to pull his sidekick away. I kicked the jackass on the floor three more times than I usually did when I wasn't trying to seriously fuck a man up, and twice as hard.

Customers rushed around us, hollering and stampeding to the door. Even through the noise, I heard a rib crack.

Music to my fucking ears.

Much as I wanted to, I couldn't pull this fucker's shades. I needed him conscious to deliver a message, especially if my guys had knocked out the other asshole.

I reached down and grabbed his jacket around his unkempt beard. "Get on your fucking feet!"

He didn't move. I shook him, readying my knee for his gut if he didn't comply.

"You don't want me to ask a second time!" I screamed. "Last chance, asshole. I'll burn this place to the fucking ground if you want to keep this fight going."

He obeyed. Told me what I wanted to hear, cradling his bloody nose.

Shatter and Blaze were at my side again, welcome reinforcements as I let him call up his boss like he said he would.

We weren't really gonna raze this place to ashes like I said, but he didn't know that. I gambled and won. The Grizzlies blinked.

Surprise and triumph kissed in my veins when he said the words. "VP says we've got an understanding…"

I was too fucking happy to waste time listening to his little threat. Now, I was gonna take my collateral and get the fuck out of here.

Didn't take me one second to think about what I wanted. I already knew. I was climbing onto the stage while the asshole who'd taken the truce bawled about it.

The girl was half-naked on one side of the stage. She covered her breasts with one arm and shot me a bitter, frightened look when I approached.

Didn't stop me. One look at her told me nothing would.

Up close, in mellower light, she was three times as hot. But her eyes were deeper, darker, filled with a sadness that made my heart ache. She shook like a scared animal when I bent, reaching for her little hand.

"What the hell do you want?"

You, babe. All fucking night. I want to see how hard I get when you're in my arms and I'm wiping away all the shitty things they've done to you.

I want to give you something beautiful you'll never forget. Not for the rest of your fucking life.

I had to bite my tongue to stop the first thing that popped into my head from spilling out.

Instead, I offered her an out. I had to get her to the clubhouse first before anything else happened.

"Get up, babe." I wondered if she'd really take my hand, but she squeezed back when my fingers wrapped around her wrist.

"I'm Maverick," I said. "President of the Prairie Devils MC, and I'm here to get you out of this shithole."

I convinced Miss Sad Eyes to ride with me. Her fragile hands were wrapped around my waist all the way down to Python.

Sure, she was afraid, but I was damn sure I could warm her up, melt whatever icy hell the Grizzlies had thrown her into.

It had been a long time since I had a project. Every time I looked at her or felt her soft fingers curling nervously around my belt, I saw my sister.

Aimee got hooked on some bad shit back home in Iowa the summer before last. Meth, pimped by a bunch of neo-Nazi trash who'd moved into my old neighborhood. I took a few weeks away from the club to get her off the junk and scream some sense into her.

It worked. Little Sis stopped turning tricks for drug money and got herself a gig helping the accountant who handles the MC's legitimate business down there.

Later, at the clubhouse, I stared at the girl. She sat by herself at the bar, slowly sipping a glass of mineral water like she was trying to shake off a bad stomach flu or something.

I had to rub my eyes. Christ. She had Aimee's expression when my sis was at her lowest, broken and debased.

That's a look a man with any brains never forgets. After Aimee, I promised myself I'd never see that soulless expression on a pretty woman again.

Not if there was anything I could do about it.

She jumped when I moved the stool next to her. I gave her a smile, and for the first time the dead-eyed sadness disappeared. Just not in the way I was expecting.

"What do you want?" she asked sourly, twisting her lips in a defensive smirk.

"I came to check up on you. You're a guest in my clubhouse, babe." I cocked my head, studying her. "Don't you want to know what happens now?"

"I really don't give a shit. Whatever it is, I know it'll be bad. And stop calling me 'babe!'" She looked at the counter, letting out a long sigh and spreading her fingertips. "Look, I learned a long time ago I don't have any choice. Not when I'm biker property. I'll do whatever it is you want."

So much for putting my curiosity to rest. I'd been expecting more of a fight. Now, I really wanted to know what the fuck had crawled underneath her skin and made such a pretty young woman spit fire.

Her tone was defiant, and her eyes glowed brighter. But the deep melancholy returned fast, painting them as black as the leather around my shoulders.

"You're not property, girl. Not anymore."

She looked up at me, blinking in surprise. I reached for her hand and squeezed it hard. I wanted to see some life, some spark.

"You're here to make sure the Grizzlies don't fuck with us again. Yeah, I'll need you to stay a little while longer for appearances. We'll give you a room here and a job if you want one. You're a guest with this MC, but if you help me out, I'll let you on your way. Wherever you want when two months are up. Most clubs never come crying for their collateral anyway."

"So, you're telling me I'm not property...except I actually am?"

She had my full attention. The girl wasn't wrong to point her finger at hypocrisy in these politics, but I was more surprised to see a little something more than apathy in her eyes.

Go ahead, babe. Fight me if it brings you back to life. I've taken my punches ever since I joined this MC. A few slaps from a girl isn't gonna do me in.

"It is what it is." I used my most serious business tone. "You work with us and everybody ends up happy. We won't treat you like shit. The Prairie Devils aren't like the Grizzlies. If you don't believe that now, tough shit. You'll figure it out soon."

No matter what I thought, I wasn't revealing shit to her until I had a handle on this bird. And speaking of 'her…'

"You got a name?"

She never looked away from me. The light in her eyes was definitely there, and I saw my stern reflection in it.

"June. Just June." She paused, drawing in a long breath. "Never June bug or June-o or Juney. If you can actually call me by my given name, then maybe I'll believe you about this place being so awesome."

"June. I can do that." I looked away for a moment, and then back. Her gaze hadn't drifted off me for a single second. "Take a few days to get your head clear. Then I'll see about getting you some work in the new place we're setting up here in Python. Sound good?"

She nodded. I muttered a goodnight and got off the stool. I watched her slowly fold her arms, protective posture in a strange place.

No way in hell she was going to my bed tonight unless I dragged her there. Fuck it. I liked a challenge.

And I'd beaten the first little part. The whole time we'd been talking, she hadn't drawn her hand out of mine until I stepped away and she drew up her arms.

Figuring her out was gonna be like a thousand piece puzzle, but the first jigsaws were wedged together.

III: Digging In (June)

For the first time in two years, I had time to think.

After my first night with the new MC, I didn't feel imminent disaster hanging over my head. These Prairie Devils were monsters, the same as every MC I'd heard of. But they were monsters with a different vibe.

I kept to myself, scheduling my runs to the bar and the little kitchen area in the back for food when nobody else was around. Maverick checked up on me a couple times a day, or else sent the big man they called Tank to do it.

I was surprised they didn't press me. Even when my sarcasm and bitchy words were sharp enough to poke an eye out.

I was a prisoner again. Surprisingly, they treated me more like a POW, and not some slave they'd torn away from her family and everything else.

God, family…

The nightmares started on my second night there. It was the same every time, reliving the awful night of Clara's defilement and death.

Come morning, I had to shake my hands to make sure the blood I saw on them in the dreams wasn't really there.

You let them rape your sister. You let them kill her. And then you erased her from your memory.

Black, bitter guilt stung at my heart. For the first time in forever, my cheeks felt hot, brutal tears trickling down.

I never cried in the Grizzles clubhouse. I wouldn't give the demons there the satisfaction of seeing me completely broken. I didn't want to admit to myself that I was.

The floodgates opened. After years of numbing, mindless survival, my brain allowed itself to feel again, and I prayed to God it wouldn't.

I almost wished Maverick and his men would do something terrible to thrust me back into survival mode. Harsh commands and backhanded blows from rough men were familiar.

I understood those threats. Surviving them was just another day.

This toxic cobra around my heart, injecting its poison into my psyche, on the other hand…

"June."

I looked up and pushed my legs together as they hung over the bed. Maverick's muscular body filled the frame leading into my room. I hadn't even heard him open the door.

"There's a little shindig tonight with food and drinks if you want to come out and have some. Fair warning: the boys'll be hitting the sauce hard. I'll make damned sure they're distracted with other women coming in. If any of my brothers get grabby with you, I'll introduce them to my fist."

I stared at him like a dumb animal. I still didn't know what to make of this man since he'd devoured me with his eyes at the Dirty Diamond.

Is this a ploy? Or is he really, truly trying to be nice?

I didn't know, and it hurt. I was too fucked up to know anything. Guess that included basic human emotion too.

"I'll think about it," I forced out the words as my brain screamed *no, no, no!*

"You do that. I'll check again before things are about to start."

I watched him turn and walk back into the hall, his heavy steps echoing to my room.

Jesus. Does he have to be so persistent? Why the fuck does he care so much about keeping tabs on me?

I've given him what he wants. Collateral. Nothing else.

Swallowing a couple sleeping pills I'd scrounged from their medical supply, I tried to force myself to sleep. Of course, I thought about Clara, and had a sick temptation to wolf down more than the standard dose.

No. You owe him a little more than a cold, dead body. It's good to owe somebody something, the first somebody who's thrown you a bone in God knows how long.

I fell into the darkness, mercifully dreamless for once.

I woke to someone shaking me. My instincts went red and I leaped up so hard I nearly whacked Maverick right on the chin.

"Whoa, June. Bad dream?"

I rolled up to sit in the darkness. He was just a faded silhouette, tall and dark and handsome. I hated to admit the last part to myself. I sure as hell wouldn't acknowledge it openly.

"What are you doing here?"

"The party's getting started." Behind his words, I heard the distant throb of music, classic rock from the nineties. "Come on out and have something to eat before my guys tear everything up."

"Maybe I will if you give me some fucking privacy."

I flushed, embarrassed at how underdressed I was when he woke me up. I was wearing shorts and a tank top.

Maverick narrowed his eyes. I couldn't tell if he was amused or annoyed. Slowly, he crossed his arms and turned around, but never left the room.

I grabbed clothes out of the closet. The MC had donated some hand-me-down stuff from locals.

I worked on my full jeans and shirt angrily, wondering why he fired me up like this.

Stupid, stupid. He probably thinks you're nuts. Since when is a stripper afraid of a man seeing her naked?

Since today. The question nagged at me while I zipped my jeans up and then tugged on a soft sweater.

"Okay," I said.

Maverick turned around. His lips gradually formed a grin when he looked me up and down.

"Very nice. Stick close by tonight, June. I'll make sure you can enjoy yourself in peace."

"I don't need a babysitter," I snapped.

His smile melted. The big biker President glared at me as I trotted past him and out into the hall.

I sensed his eyes on me the whole time, as intense as they'd been the night he took me from the Dirty Diamond.

Was it lust in his x-ray heat or annoyance? I wish I knew.

I wondered, but I didn't dare look back. I couldn't handle that shit right now, no matter how much it let me feel something besides the darkness in my heart.

This MC ate much better than anything I'd seen with the Grizzlies. The Prairie Devils had huge racks of prime rib and snacks laid out on a big table. The small area around the bar was full of men in leather and women who'd come in from town.

I chewed my meat and vegetables anxiously as my eyes wandered through the crowd.

Life here was different, all right. There was no stomach knotting tension, no snide remarks, and none of the damning looks I'd seen with the Grizzlies.

Maverick's buddies carried on with each other like old friends. They laughed and slapped fists, making the rafters shake with their crude jokes and wild catcalls to the ladies.

"New girl. I was starting to wonder if you were a vampire." I looked up and saw a man who looked a lot like Maverick, except leaner and a little younger.

It was his VP, Blaze. I squinted at him, confused.

"You're up among the living, eating with us. Happy to see it."

Fuck you, I wanted to say. But giving myself a worse reputation than I likely already had with these guys wasn't appealing just yet.

"Why aren't you drinking and finding a girl?" I gave him my best *leave-me-alone* bitch voice.

No luck. Blaze pulled out the chair across from me and sat down, crossing his hands. I saw his fingers were filled with big, heavy rings bearing the MC's letters.

"I like to be totally comfortable before I let my hair down." A joke. His hair was medium length and well kept, much like Maverick, and I wasn't laughing. "I want to know what your plans are after we're done keeping you."

Very direct. He got my attention. I wondered how much I could get away with by offering him something.

"Only if you tell me a little about this place. I'd like to know more about your President."

"Maverick?" His eyes widened and he tilted his head, too fascinated for my liking. "Aaron's my brother. I don't mean that in the MC way either. Half-brothers from the same momma who grew up in a dusty town in Iowa together. Been a Nomad his whole adult life and President for years. He's led us through shit that would make your skin crawl."

"Try me." I showed my teeth, but it wasn't a smile.

"No thanks. You're right to wonder about him. Personally, I wonder why the hell he chose you out of the other girls there that night, and why he's still putting up with your piss poor attitude. Let me tell you something about Maverick…"

I looked away, shocked at the way he flung the attitude back in my face.

"He's a fucking tiger. Once he sinks his teeth and claws into something, he doesn't let up. He can be your best friend, or a man you most definitely do *not* wanna piss off. He's a patient man. He'll wait until the time's just right to do it, and then he'll strike."

"Jeez," I raised my hands defensively. "I didn't mean it like that. If he's the tiger around here, then what does that make you?"

"The asshole," Blaze said, leaning forward a little. "Just like any VP should be, doing the dirty work the President can't. Or won't. Right now, I've told you what you wanted and then some. Your turn. Tell me what your intentions are."

I cringed.

"I'm counting down the days 'til I'm out of your fucking hair. I want to blow this town, this state, and never look back," I lied, but at least I had real energy behind it to sound convincing. "Seattle. Maybe Portland. I've never been to a big city before, and it seems as good a place as any to get lost and start over."

There. Satisfied?

Blaze nodded. "Sounds reasonable. You're not the only one who wants to blow this little mountain town. We're Nomads, and Nomads need to ride free once our job here's finished. You remember that before you think twice about getting under my brother's skin, or hell, anywhere below his belt."

I shot him a nasty smile and hissed through my teeth. Couldn't believe he'd said it.

Asshole was right.

Blaze shot up and didn't bother to push his chair in. He walked back to the group, hanging with a couple younger guys with the Prairie Devils patch.

I sat alone, finishing my food. Shaking my head, I wondered what the hell I'd been thinking coming out here at Maverick's request.

This was a place where I didn't belong. Their brotherhood wasn't meant for me.

Hell, maybe I ought to give serious thought to Portland or Seattle. If only I weren't clueless about anything the real world had to offer besides shaking my ass for perverts and criminal bikers.

I waited until the night drew longer. Several guys abandoned their bottles and dragged the local sluts to their rooms, or else hauled them onto their bikes and drove to the apartments they were renting.

I emptied my mineral water and filled my glass with whiskey. The amber fire ran down my throat, soothing everything in the sweet forgetfulness it offered.

Its soft glow made me forget all about being damaged, bitchy, unwanted June.

The liquor hit hard on a near empty stomach. I'd eaten slowly, and not very much. Time began to blur and the stuff found that sweet spot in my brain, stroking me through my misery until I purred.

"What's going on? You having a good time?"

It was hard to make my eyes focus on Maverick. I grabbed the bottle with both hands, afraid he'd take it away from me.

"I think you've had your fill," he said, pulling it away.

"No, I'm almost twenty-one. I swear, lemme show you my license…" I slurred the last word.

"Babe, I don't give a shit about you being a few months under the legal limit. I do care about how you're gonna blast yourself into a hangover, and how that's gonna fuck with the pills you're taking to go to sleep."

I sat up straight through my drunken haze, wrinkling my face. "Huh? How the hell do you know about those?"

"I'm an MC President, June. I'd be doing a shitty job if I didn't notice pills missing from our medicine cabinet, or figure out they're the reason I almost had to pour cold water on your face to get you up this evening."

"Fuck!" I sputtered. I just knew I'd find the little boxes gone from underneath my pillow later too. "Why's it any of your business what I do? Why can't you leave me alone when I'm doing exactly what you wanted? I came to your stupid party, didn't I?"

He leaned in closer to me, so close I could smell his scent. Spicy, strong, and masculine. A strange bolt of interest shot through me, but I blamed it on the whiskey clouding my mind.

"Because a screwed up girl who's sick from drugs – or worse, a junkie – is no fucking good to me. I kick problems in the ass before they become serious business. Right now, this MC has got its hands full. I don't need to find you dead some morning when Shatter makes the breakfast call…"

Clara flashed in my mind. I shook my head, suppressing the vile memory.

"Sorry I'm such a nuisance. I already told your brother, I'll be outta your hair whenever you let me go. Won't waste a second longer here."

"You said that to Blaze? Nosy bastard." His face softened, and then tightened angrily. "Look, you're reading this shit all wrong. I want you to get on your feet while you're with us. Remember, I'm the one who chose you as fucking collateral. Nobody else."

"Shoulda picked a different girl. Guess nobody told you the Dirty Diamond's star dancer is also the most fucked up."

He snorted, picked up the glass at his side, and slammed his whiskey. Maverick stood, leaning far over the bar, and came up a minute later with a glass of something clear in hand.

"Mineral water. Your favorite. Drink this and show me you care about waking up alive tomorrow."

I reluctantly accepted the drink. It tasted cool on my lips.

Through the empty prism top of the glass, I studied him. Maverick was cold, hard, and demanding. But so far, he hadn't been cruel.

He was a lawless savage. It must've been the drink and my bleeding heart that caused the sudden desire surging through my body. An image flashed before my eyes, so vivid and scorching I nearly dropped my water.

I imagined his huge body wedged between my legs, naked and plastered with the tattoos I could only see the edges of around his clothes. He pulled me to him with the same fevered need in his commands, roaming his big paws all over my body, grabbing my flesh and taking whatever he wanted.

Stop it! Now you remember why you didn't drink around the Grizzlies?

I did. Of course, thinking about fucking one of them made me wretch. Contrasting Maverick with my old captors made him much, much more appealing too.

And that was dangerous…

"Good girl," he said when my empty glass clinked on the counter. "Our new skin shop opens next week in town. Think you got it in you to get back on the stage? You'll keep way more money working for me than you ever did those assholes."

"Sure." God help me, I leaned in closer to him as I said it, really tasting his rich manly scent for the first time.

Sweat. Leather. Whiskey. Power.

"Good. With you debuting there, you're sure to help the place get on its fucking legs. Half the guys we've talked to in this town say they drove up to Missoula just to see you. Not real hard to see why."

He looked me up and down. My panties drowned with wet heat, forced out as his eyes crawled over my flushed skin.

I was losing control, and it felt good. Damned good.

Where the hell had the shrieking bitch gone? Was she really put down so easy by a few shots?

"You know, I've seen hundreds of guys watching me shake my thing. But nobody watched me the way you did that night."

"Yeah?"

The air between us swarmed with heat and pheromones. Maverick recognized the animal glint in my eyes and threw his arms around me at once, jerking me onto his lap.

Holy shit. What's happening? Why can't I stop?

The mutinous nub between my legs pulsed, sending rough, filthy fire straight up my core. It was like two years of pent up frustration boiled over at once.

I shouldn't have been surprised. A young girl can only hold her body under the big, sexy gun without going further for so long. I just never expected I'd throw myself at a biker – not a man like the brutes who'd wrecked my life.

Was I that fucked up?

It sure didn't feel like it with his hot breath on me. Maverick leaned in, one little touch away from fusing his lips to mine. I wondered if he'd taste as good as he smelled.

"You like being watched, babe?" He was only an inch away, running the very tip of his tongue over his bottom lip.

Hearing him call me 'babe' didn't upset me anymore. It had a nice ring to it in his deep, slightly smoky, and very manly voice.

"I like touching more." Crap. I almost said *fucking*, but then I would've sounded like a complete and total slut.

His hands tightened around me. *Good,* I thought.

Let him think I'm a wounded little birdie if it gives me this heat, this sweet distraction. Hell, maybe I need to let go a little. I need something new to take away the memories.

I wasn't a tiny girl, but Maverick was huge. His hands traveled lower down my back, stopping on my hips to squeeze and throw me forward.

My legs went around his waist, and I sensed the very edge of a raging hard-on below his jeans. My hips bucked instantly, grinding against him.

"Fuck!" he whispered, pressing one hand behind my head.

No more screwing around. He pulled me into him, and his lips were on mine. It was a world shattering a kiss, a kiss so wicked and intense it caused me to short circuit.

I moaned into his sweet lips, running my tongue across them. Next thing I knew, I had a sensation like I was going to faint.

Seriously. I'd only had the disembodied feeling a couple times, as if all the blood in my system had pooled below the waist and was now rushing to my head at once.

I literally swooned in his arms. Maverick lunged forward, aiming for another kiss, but he must've felt the way I'd gone limp in his arms.

"June? Babe?" No answer. "Fuck!"

He threw my head against his shoulder and stroked my back. I cooed, loving the cool contrast of his leather jacket and the scratchy heat of his stubble.

My head throbbed, cycling through pain and pleasure and fear. Mainly exhaustion. My adrenals were shot for the night, fogged by whiskey and completely spent from all the shitty and amazing things that just happened out here.

"You better not pass out on me," he said sternly.

His hands were on my thighs again, but not to claim me. He lifted me up, safe against his chest. I rolled my face against him, trying not to cry as he began to walk.

"I'm gonna let you down," he whispered. "Take it easy. Roll over."

I was on my side in the squeaky old bed. I shifted at his words, throwing one arm over my face. God, I needed total darkness, hoping the mineral water and some sleep would do its thing to shake the worst hangover of my life.

I slept fitfully. At some point in the night, I rolled, and cracked my eyes.

The other side of the bed was being held down by one hell of a weight. It took me a minute to realize the weight was Maverick.

Holy shit!

In the peaceful darkness, he looked beautiful while he slept. And still in control too, if the fierce tattooed arm around my waist was any indication.

I rolled into him, nestling against his shoulder. Muscles deep inside me clenched, slick with desire, but the sickly headache forced me to ignore them.

When I cracked my eyes again, the bed was cold and empty.

I threw my hand out, rubbing the space where he'd left his impression. It was morning – maybe even noon. Pale gray light filled the room through the half-open blinds attached to my window.

I threw my legs over the bed and sat up.

Big mistake. My stomach flipped so hard I almost lost last night's dinner all over my bed.

My shaking foot touched something on the floor. I reached for it, and saw it was another bottle of water.

I drank it in shallow sips, thinking about him the whole time.

Something amazing had happened – or rather, almost happened – last night.

Frankly, it scared the hell out of me.

In the fresh dull light, I remembered who I was. A man like Maverick would always be a bastard biker, no matter how big and gorgeous and caring he might be.

God, had I really almost fucked him?

I saw myself in the small mirror across the room. I looked like a fucking mess – hair rumpled, red faced, clothes wrinkled with last night's sweat.

Ugly. Just like the way I'd acted last night, the way I'd come damnably close to doing something I'd regret for the last of my life.

I chugged the rest of the water and threw the empty bottle on the floor. My stomach growled, but I ignored it. I didn't dare risk creeping out of my room and running into *him.*

Limp hand over heart, I swore off drinking, and not just due to the hangover. The same darkness I'd carried since Clara's death lashed inside me, insistent and unsettled.

I couldn't use whiskey to keep it contained, and I sure as hell couldn't use big, tattooed, dangerous men either. I needed something a lot more powerful to drown my demons.

IV: Missing Pieces (Maverick)

My cock kept jerking in my pants at church the next day. A wicked heat shot through me like a big swig of Jack. It took all my energy to focus, everything I fucking had to forget about the way I'd slept next to that beautiful fallen angel last night.

So close. So fucking close to her skin, her little ass, her sweet, tight pussy.

I'd been a perfect gentleman. Fucking girls when they were screwed up and unconscious wasn't any fun.

Settling in next to her and behaving was far from easy. Had to run back to the bar for another pint of Jack and a bottle of water before I joined her in bed.

The whiskey was to make sure I didn't do anything fucking stupid. The water was for her. She'd need a lot more than the lone glass I'd served up at the bar to get through the day.

Now, it had been three days and she'd gone back to her cat-like ways, only scurrying out for food at night. I hoped like hell she didn't have any regrets.

"Well, what do you think, brother?" Blaze stared at me.

I looked up, wondering how many times he'd repeated the question. "Sounds like we're in business. I'll talk to June as soon as we adjourn and make sure she's feeling up to it tomorrow."

"She better be," Blaze growled. "Girl's the god damned star. We've spent plenty giving her ass a place to crash too."

Anger throbbed through me. My eyes focused on him, and I forgot about June's tight little body pressed up against me for a micro-second.

"Cut her some slack. She's been through a lot, and I don't think she'll let us down." I wasn't asking.

Time to puff out the Prez patch and bitch slap my boys back into line, including my blood brother.

Blaze's face went cold. He wore the look that said, *are you fucking kidding me?*

I wasn't in the mood to argue with my asshole brother. MC code meant I didn't have to. I was the President of this god damned club, and it didn't matter if the patches on my cut said PYTHON or NOMADS.

I never went looking for a wrestling match with my brothers, but I'd remind anybody who forgot what I was the hard way.

The other guys shifted uncomfortably. Hypno and Shatter had been around long enough to know when to stay out of it. The new guy, on the other hand, sat there like an expressionless gorilla.

I honestly couldn't tell what the fuck was turning in his head.

"Hey, Tank," I said, snapping my fingers for extra emphasis. "You've been on guard duty before, right?"

He nodded. "Sure thing. Throttle had me escorting the guys on mule duty all winter. Also guarded my fair share of shit in Afghanistan before I left the service."

"Then you're taking the first shift at the new joint. Just seeing a guy like you should be enough to keep any uppity bastards in line."

No joke. In all my time as President, I'd learned it was a lot easier to prevent a fight from starting by flexing than actually throwing punches after it began.

"You got it, boss. Uh, what's the new place gonna be called?"

I almost smacked my head. The muscle head across the table had a great point nobody else had considered.

We'd finished everything with this new strip joint except the name, saving it for last.

"It'll be right next to the new tattoo parlor. How about Pink and Ink?" Hypno piped up.

"That's shit, brother. We need something spicy...maybe Cinnamon Swing or something?" Shatter was always trying to one-up Hypno. They'd both transferred into the Nomads at the same time.

Blaze just shook his head. I stroked my chin, putting some serious thought into it. The name wasn't just gonna be on the neon sign and the billboards stretching out to Bozeman and Coeur d'Alene.

We were the owners. And like everything with club credibility, the place's reputation fucking mattered.

"I like the pink part for everything it implies," I said, pausing as Hypno and Shatter snickered. "Let's keep the motherfucker simple. Pink Unlimited."

The two guys who'd weighed in squinted. Tank stretched his hands in front of him, disinterested in the naming part and only wanting to know where he'd end up.

"It'll do," Blaze said. "We've already decked the fucking place in pink anyway."

"Doesn't sound like we need a vote." I waited, and nobody disagreed.

Even mundane shit gave them voting rights as long as it was club business. I'd been head long enough for democracy to get under my skin, and I welcomed the times when everything went through seamlessly.

"Do you want us to start pushing shit on opening night? I hear the mule's coming through tonight. Throttle wouldn't blink if he dropped off some extra dope here, yeah?" Hypno asked. "Could be lucrative. This fucking place is dry as a bone except for the shit the Grizzlies used to push down here, or so the locals say..."

I leaned back in my chair. Fucking charmer. He was doing his thing – the very thing that gave him his name.

Some family drama with Hypno and his estranged family made him hard up for money. He wanted to start raking it in right away, and he was trying to charm up support from the other members to get it over my stubborn head.

Hypno could be one cool, calculating prick, and his road name was a reminder to the rest of us not to be fooled by his hypnotic shit. On the plus side, when he aimed it at everybody outside the club, they were truly fucked by his cool charm.

"The Prairie Devils aren't in the business of dealing anything, brother. You know that. We just run the shit and take a cut off both ends for playing middle man. Throttle would have my ass for dinner if I got the Fed's eyes on this club doing the one thing we don't do."

"Okay." Hypno spread his hands, hoping to deflect a lecture. "We're cool, Prez. Just thought things might be different out here…"

Yeah. I'll bet you did.

"No other business?" I waited, silently relieved when five seconds went by without anything from the other guys. "Then let's call it an evening and get our last ducks in a row. It's all about opening up Pink Unlimited now."

I slammed my fists on the table. Most MC Presidents had gavels, but the idea of lugging around a fucking mallet as a Nomad hadn't ever been appealing.

I enjoyed using my hands. Damned fine way to keep my knuckles warm and ready at a moment's notice too.

It was late when I went looking for June. Had to bust ass all evening with a few last calls to the county to make sure everything was kosher for opening night at the strip club.

I took a quick shot at the bar and then walked down the hall. I knocked at her door, but there wasn't any answer. Reaching for the knob, I gave it a good turn.

Unlocked. I pushed it open to stick my head inside and saw her bed was empty.

Weird. Girl's been avoiding me and everybody else since party night.

I looked high and low through the bar, the kitchen, and even the little storage rooms. She was nowhere.

I started to wonder if she'd done something stupid like run. The idea of her leaving us, leaving *me*, when I'd been so fucking close to getting my hands on her turned my hands into fists.

Fuck. No, babe, don't fucking do this to me. Not now.

The back door practically tore off its hinges as I went outside. I stepped into the darkness, walked past the Harleys, listening to the still night.

No, scratch that. Not so still.

The voices around the corner drew me in. I saw her, standing next to the tall older guy who blew in a few hours earlier from Cassandra.

"I don't care how much you're offering, girl. I don't push the hard shit unless my Prez tells me to. Now, fuck off." Bolt sounded angry.

What the fuck was going on here? I stomped toward them, stepping right between our guest and June. Didn't like his tone with her one bit.

"Hey, brother, this girl's under my fucking watch. If she's done something to ruffle your feathers then you better let me know about it. Keeping my people in line is Python business. Not Cassandra's."

Bolt tightened his lips and cocked his head, sizing me up. "Jesus, Maverick. Your whore needs a tighter leash."

I stepped forward, using my size to push him toward the wall. "June's not a club whore. Watch your fucking mouth. I don't appreciate dumb assumptions, brother. Now, what the fuck is going on here?"

"She was pestering me for a hit. Wanted to buy some of the shit in my bag. I offered her a couple joints, but she was interested in the smack. Wouldn't take no for an answer the first two times, and everybody knows I don't do three strikes."

Fuck. Did the party knock something loose in her head, or is she trying to fucking defy me?

I turned so fast I nearly pushed the asshole messenger in front of me to the floor. Rage prickled in my blood. Felt the hair on the back of my neck standing up like a werewolf's.

"It's true?"

June's face was red, contorted. She wouldn't look at me, staring at the ground instead. She shuffled her feet and gave me the smallest, mousiest nod ever.

I looked over my shoulder at Bolt. "Beat it. I need to talk to her alone."

"No arguments here."

I waited until he was gone. Then I was on her, grabbing her by the shoulders and hauling her feet off the ground.

She kicked at my shins. I was fucking pissed. Her little toe taps felt like pebbles bouncing around my boots when I'm riding on a gravel road.

I carried her three steps to the wall and pinned her down. June looked shocked, scared, but offended more than anything else.

Motherfucking offended. You have no right, babe.

"Did the Jack blast away your memory of what happened the other night, or what?" I demanded.

"I just wanted to forget. You took away my sleeping pills...I can't work if I'm thinking about all the bad shit that's happened to me, Maverick. You want me on the stage tomorrow, don't you?"

"Bullshit!" I roared. "I don't need a whacked out junkie grinding on my fucking stage. You got a single clue in your pretty little head what that shit does to a person?"

Her face softened. Familiar dark sadness filled her eyes like stars going out one by one.

"Yeah. I do. My mother was hooked..."

My grip relaxed one iota. I snorted, wondering if I was hearing this right.

"Then you're even fucking crazier than I thought."

I let go, but kept her pinned with my body, tossing one hand through my hair. "Dammit, June. You're not gonna piss your life away on a death watch while I'm looking over your shoulder. Here's what's gonna happen – "

She flinched. Seeing her hurt and shamed activated all my guardian instincts. Wasn't easy protecting her from her own fucking self this time.

"Look at me, June. Not at the fucking ground." I waited until I had her absolute attention, even as a few hot tears slipped from her eyes. "Tomorrow, I'm gonna watch you shake your sweet ass on the stage for the whole town. And then you're going in the background to make sure every other girl we've hired brings in the bucks."

"What?" Confusion shined in her eyes.

"Tomorrow's your last dance, babe. Make it a good one. You've got enough years under your belt to train in other girls and make sure the fucking place runs smooth as velvet."

"That's like...a promotion." She shook her head in disbelief. "Why? Why do you trust me to do anything?"

"Being a manager is all about responsibilities. You're responsible for the supplies, the financials, the girls – everything goes through you before it gets to me, and it better be good."

She trembled a little beneath me. Fuck, it didn't take much for her to get me hard, even when my heart was pumping with fury instead of lust.

"I'm also putting you in charge so you can't fuck up again. Keeping your hands busy is the best way I know to keep tabs on you. A junkie pole dancing can hide her bad habits a lot longer than a junkie balancing receipts."

"Okay…I don't have to be told twice." She looked serious, but she'd fooled me once. I wasn't buying it a second time without ramming things home.

I stepped up, sandwiching her between me and the brick wall, feeling her amazing tits plush against my chest. Shit, her nipples were hard, which only made my cock harder.

Not now, dammit. You'll get your fill of her pretty body tomorrow.

"Then do it without me telling you anything else. If you fuck up and I get wind of you doing dope, smack, Jack, or fucking aspirin, I'll have your ass laid across my lap and beat it raw. And believe me, babe, I won't give a shit just how sweet it looks when I'm in the mood to set things straight."

I tore myself away. She slumped, her knees giving way. I took her wrist in one hand hard and helped pull her up until she was steady.

"Go inside and get your shit together. You've got about twenty hours before the grand opening."

I knew June's last dance would be fucking amazing. But nothing prepared me for actually seeing her up there opening night.

Everybody except Blaze turned out to cut the proverbial ribbon. Not just because we wanted to make sure it was smooth sailing, but because we needed to make sure the Grizzlies kept their word. Those fucks could cause a lot of pain and embarrassment if they decided to hit our new business on opening night.

The other guys were making their rounds and helping the two bouncers we'd hired. I sat front stage with a straight whiskey in my hand.

No ice. Didn't need anything taking the edge off Jack's sweet, familiar fire.

The older part-time lady working costumes and makeup came out and said a few words of introduction. Then the lights flipped, darkening the whole lounge and painting the stage in silver and gold tinsel light.

Some fancy electronic tune switched on. The curtain opened and Junes stepped out, naked as the day she was born, except for two tiny golden clamshells pushing up her tits and a matching thong wedged between her ass.

And fuck – what an ass! I nearly spilled Jack all over my dick, which sprang up the instant I saw her.

Worse, she was looking right at me, never breaking her gaze once to look over the hushed crowd. June moistened her lips with her tongue and lunged at the pole, grabbing it with both hands.

Her ass swung, thrusting as she went, around and around. The girl moved like a god damned wildcat, sleek and fast and beautiful.

Would've made me dizzy if I didn't break my eyes away to look past her ass. Thank God there was plenty to see elsewhere on her fine body. And the way she moved what she owned – *Jesus H. Christ.*

She twirled, locking her lush legs around the pole. Her hips ground against it, and when she turned another few degrees, her back was to me and I had a perfect view of her ass. Sliding up and down the stiff metal, she teased it with her voluptuous cheeks like a great big maypole.

Didn't take a college degree to know what that shit symbolized.

"Fuck," I muttered to myself.

My cock strained horribly in my pants. For a second, I was worried I'd lose my load like a fucking high school kid on prom night.

I shook my head, clenching my jaw. Had to keep control.

I couldn't deny this babe had real, raw, crazy fucking power. Under any other circumstances I would've thought not having pussy for a few weeks had something to do with it.

Being back in Iowa to help out Aimee put me through a similar dry spell. I was going fucking nuts until I hit the local watering hole one night after sis was passed out asleep, and bedded the first hot chick I could find.

I thought about that romp, remembered how I hauled her onto my bike and threw her head over my shoulder, dragging her off to the ratty hotel like a caveman. Only this girl didn't hold a tiny fucking candle to June.

The clam shell came off. She licked her lips – hissing raw desire through her teeth I swore I heard over the booming music and jeers – and grabbed her breasts in both hands.

The men went nuts when she let her girls bounce, squeezing her nipples while she rubbed up and down that pole.

The hoots and hollers of all the other boys there made me see red. I wanted to kill everybody else in the room and claim her for myself.

Seriously.

Good thing the hard-on I was popping wouldn't let me stand up. Not for anything.

My brothers knew to keep their distance while they ogled her too. I had a feeling Blaze wasn't the only one who sensed my little attraction. Had to be the only reason why nobody else had tried to bed her yet, especially without any regular whores to fuck in the clubhouse.

June bounced, her sweet tits wobbling with her, sending the same delicious vibration through her full hips.

God damn, woman. I felt those fucking words in my bones.

It's not every day you see a woman with her figure. My cock jerked again, tangling my boxers against my fly.

Easy, easy. We're gonna have her. Soon.

We're gonna lay fucking claim to this girl and make it official too. After tonight, every other asshole in Python's gonna want a piece of her. Maybe even my own brothers.

And I couldn't do shit to stop them either except defend my woman and make her an old lady. Until then, it was technically open season, and anybody in the MC could court her, from patched in members to our local hang arounds.

But June wouldn't give herself up easy. She'd made that crystal-fucking-clear.

I wondered if she had such a chip on her shoulder because those Grizzlies assholes raped her.

Just the thought of it turned my fingers into fists, ready for gore.

June walked away from the pole, towards the stage's very edge. The lights shifted as she bent, popping her ass out. She reached up and undid the little hook holding her gold panties on.

They fell to the floor and the loudest, bawdiest cheers I'd ever heard exploded. She looked through her stretched legs, and even when her pretty face was upside down, she found me.

I must've looked like a stupid fucking teen seeing tits and ass for the very first time. She shocked me, paralyzed me with pure fire, made my drink shake in my hand as I fought the urge not to rip her off the stage and throw her onto my lap.

Her hips twitched. She was wagging them right at me, sweet cheeks and wet pussy and all.

Everything. Won't rest until I've had my hands on all that, and a whole lot more too.

"Fuck." I completely lost track how many times I'd whispered my trademark phrase.

Didn't know and didn't fucking care. I forced my glass up to my mouth and slammed the last shot of whiskey in my tumbler.

Hot relief hit my guts. I had about thirty seconds before the toasty warmth would hit my cock and make me burn even hotter for her.

I blinked. People were clapping and the lights were flashing.

June was at center stage, one hand on the nearest pole. For the first time, I saw her smile, a soft and mellow curl on her lips that wasn't darkened by the sadness in her eyes.

Hell, by her standards, she looked happy. Sad, but happy.

Fucking paradox or not, that's exactly what she was.

She waved with skimpy panties in hand and then disappeared. I caught one last glimpse of her pretty ass disappearing behind the curtain.

My brain went wild with all the sick, sweet, and wild things I wanted to do to her. I wanted to absolutely bury myself in her flesh and not come up for weeks.

I needed to taste her, feel her, fuck her to stay sane. This wasn't just a skin crush. This was a fucking lust storm electrifying my blood, and it wouldn't stop until I was buried in June balls deep.

Other girls came out and danced. They were pretty, but they didn't do shit for the rock hard boner in my pants.

Not like her.

This hard-on belonged to June. All my steel lust went to her. I kept thinking about her the whole night as more Jack flowed into my glass and whiskey dick finally tamed the missile in my pants.

I let the poison cool in my system. When I wasn't pissing drunk, I stood and walked backstage, past the small gaggle of girls laughing and stretching their legs on their break.

"Hey, big boy. You're the one who set this place up, aren't you?" A leggy blonde got up and stood in my path.

She leaned into me, throwing her arms around me. She was okay, the kinda easy, pretty pussy I would've hauled back to my room on a normal night.

But nothing about this night was ordinary anymore. Not since I saw June giving her fans one fuck of a send off, taunting me with her hourglass perfection.

"Get off me," I said gruffly, pushing her aside.

The blonde toppled back to the flimsy chair she'd been sitting on and looked at me in shock. I flashed her my best warning look and shook my head.

"That's not what I'm paying you for. I'm paying you to look alive and shake your ass the best you can out there. Don't you forget it. The MC writes your checks, ladies, and I'm its President."

She nodded respectfully, and then I was gone, stepping over a few crushed cigarette cartons and robes some girls had left on the floor.

June was in a little cubicle, combing her hair in the mirror. I held in a genuine fucking gasp when I saw she was naked. The girl hadn't bothered to put a lick of clothing on since her last dance.

She noticed my silhouette in the mirror. I watched her turn, baring her knock out tits without any shyness.

"Guess I can't whine about not knocking when there aren't any doors, huh?"

I smiled and shook my head. "Guess not. I wanted to come by and tell you what an awesome job you did out there tonight. Didn't exactly get to enjoy your show the first time I saw you."

"Well, I'm glad you liked it. The deal's still on, right? Making me manager and all?" She threw her long dark hair over one breast.

"Count on it. Time for you to bury June the ass shaker, and let June the brass tacks businesswoman out."

A crooked smile crossed her face. I knew she was unsure of herself, and the uncertainty in her expression made her look even cuter.

Fuck, there was that hard on again. Rigid and angry as ever, pulsing in my pants.

"So, is that all you came by to tell me, or did you show up to ogle me too?"

This girl. This fucking mouth.

"More than that." I stepped up to her and leaned down, picking her beautiful naked body up and throwing her head over my shoulder.

She squealed and actually laughed. Her little fists beat on my back until I marched her over by the mirror and sat her on her feet again.

"What the fuck, Maverick?"

I reached to the floor and scooped up the shirt and jeans she'd tossed in a heap. "Throw these on and come with me. I'm taking you back to the clubhouse."

June dressed like I asked, turning her back to me. I watched her normal black panties go up and hug her sweet ass. All the sweeter for me to tear away again later.

When she finished, she turned toward me. I extended a hand to take hers, but she didn't return the grip.

Fine, I thought. *Looks like we get to do this the fun way.*

"Come here, babe." I scooped her up in my arms, carrying her like a kitten.

She fought me with little curses and sighs the whole time. But the way she blushed and clammed up when we went by her new employees – the other strippers – told me she was into it.

I settled her on my bike without so much as a "fuck you."

"Been a long time since I've had you on my Harley. Hold on tight, babe. It's a cold night."

No shit. The waning afterglow of whiskey in my joints reminded me just how cool it was. I made damned sure I was good to drive before climbing onto my ride with her.

June's hands were wrapped around my sides. Tentative at first, but when we got on the road, she clenched me harder, lower, smoothing her hands out to hold onto my abs.

Suddenly, the cold wasn't so bad after all. It caused her to nestle closely, resting her pretty head on my shoulder.

Even twenty miles out from the bed where I'd take her, the sexual fusion between us was obvious. Her legs touched the back of my hips, spread wide and inviting.

Fuck. I grunted, clenching my handlebars tight as we rode along the pitch black mountain road.

My cock wouldn't stop twitching. Especially when we rounded the next bend and I felt her fingers edging lower, sweeping beneath my belt in little strokes to graze my upper thigh, painfully close to the hard-on waiting for her in the middle.

Nothing, nothing, nothing was gonna stop me from claiming her good and proper tonight.

Not even hitting a fucking bear or a mountain goat in the night. If I wasn't balls deep in June's tight wet cunt in the next ten minutes, then it meant the world had ended.

She moaned softly in my ear over the engine's growl. It had been a long time since my bike's vibrations really got to me in a sexual way, but shit, this little ride sexualized damned near everything I touched.

Only God himself could've stopped me from laying her out and driving into her. The raw, primal pulse between my legs wouldn't fucking stop one second for anything else.

V: Corralled (June)

We rode through the darkness.

I wondered what the hell was happening to me. The fever I'd felt the other night when I was drunk and pressed up against him had returned tenfold.

Not that I hadn't fanned it myself.

The whole time I was up on the stage, I took off my clothes for him, and only him. I couldn't remember ever smiling during an act before, even when men were piling up dirty dollars at my feet.

But tonight, he got me doing things the old June never would've done while she was owned by the Grizzlies.

Just the idea of *wanting* to be owned by someone else scared the hell out of me. It also put my senses on red hot alert, sending an electric shock through my veins.

And the current was only getting sharper as I hugged him tight, warming myself against his big biker back in the cold springtime night.

His muscles were hard as stone beneath my fingertips. I pressed against the shirt he wore beneath his cut, inhaling his trademark scent.

Musk and traces of whiskey assaulted my nose. His bike vibrated between my legs, making me hotter and wetter than I already was for this man.

The roar echoed in the helmet covering my ears. Only I wasn't sure if it was really just the engine anymore or the loud, relentless desire screaming inside me, making everything from head to toe buzz with a want so fierce it hurt.

I felt him up while we rode, and I wanted to feel more. Every sweep of my fingers beneath his belt caused him to grind backward a little more, bringing us closer and satisfying my hungry flesh.

We jerked to a stop in front of the clubhouse. I sat up, surprised. Hadn't even realized we were back.

I'd been too focused on his hard, rough feel beneath my hands and the Harley's comforting drone.

I looked up, reaching to undo my helmet. Must've been too slow for Maverick because he cupped my chin with one hand and yanked on the strap.

"Let's go, babe. I already told you the next time I get your ass beneath me, it isn't gonna be soft or slow. I'm not fucking waiting a second longer."

He tore me up from the Harley's seat. The clubhouse was mostly deserted except for Blaze at the bar. He ignored us, giving all his attention to the beer in his hand and the race on the TV.

Maverick carried me right past my own room. My heart beat faster when I realized we were heading for his, the makeshift home he'd set up.

Did he even have a real home? I wondered if he understood the word at all as a Nomad, or if he was a drifter like me.

One quick push of the door and we were inside. He kicked the heavy wood shut behind him and clicked the lock.

A lamp flickered to life. Its cover was made out of green, red, and blue stained glass, casting an unearthly low glow through the room.

His room was neat and simple. Nothing but a bed, a small desk, and a few knickknacks holding pictures and Prairie Devils MC symbols.

About what I expected for an MC President. Especially a Nomad.

My back hit the bed. I instantly spread myself out, clinging to his neck. Maverick detected the surging need in my touch and swept in for a kiss.

He covered my small body with his. And his kiss came rough, just like the first time. He pushed his tongue past my lips and went searching for mine, teasing softly before he found what he wanted and thrust in and out.

I moaned. I forgot to breathe, and then I panicked and bit him on the lip a little, struggling for fresh air.

"Ah, fuck, June. I had a feeling you'd be a biter." He pulled back, a wicked grin on his face. "Just you be careful, babe. Whatever you give me, I'll give it back twice as fucking rough. I'm gonna light you on fire."

His hands reached for my hips. I pushed against him, but it only ripped my jeans down faster.

My legs twisted around his, searching for his warmth. My body wasn't listening to the last little storms of doubt in my brain.

It was way ahead of the game. Those last whining voices disappeared the instant his stubble raked across my bare neck, followed by his lips.

"Oh! Jesus!" I dug my nails into his lower neck, panting as I rose.

His rough, calloused hands went up my bare legs. He circled them behind my thighs, cupped my ass, and squeezed my cheeks through my panties.

I almost turned into a puddle right there, beneath him. Certainly, everything beneath the waist did, turning into nothing but heat and cream.

Maverick kept one hand on my ass and reached for my shirt. He guided my arms over my head and ripped it off in one jerk, savage need spilling from his eyes.

And both those deadly, serious eyes were fixed on my half-naked body. I gushed, unashamed for once at how excited his killer expression made me.

Just a few weeks earlier, I would've been revolted and terrified if Vulture or any of his men looked at me like Maverick watched me now. But Maverick wasn't the demon I thought, and warm desire flickered beneath his animal need, feeding the wildfire only he could extinguish.

Hands went behind my back, and he practically tore my bra strap in the rush to get it off. I didn't care. I helped the cups away and flung the garment across the room.

He kissed me deep, and then hooked both hands near my panties again. I screamed and throbbed when he tore them down past my knees.

They didn't glide. They flew, dangerously close to getting shredded around my ankles in the process.

He leaned into my naked flesh, kissing and sucking. His jeans pushed against my bare slit hard.

I arched my back, moaning loudly and rocking. He silenced me with another kiss, thrusting his tongue in and out of my mouth, need growing with every wet stroke.

He took one nipple in his hand and pinched it between his fingers. My whole body jerked, rocking into his bulge harder.

God, I needed him inside me fucking soon, or I wasn't going to survive. I literally burned between my legs for him, a violent ache so hot it was painful.

He grunted, breaking the latest kiss. His hands went to my hips and held me down, moving me away from rocking against his cock.

"Not just yet, babe. I like to feel and taste what I'm gonna fuck first…"

"But I want you!"

He ignored me, prolonging my agony. Finally, I got relief when he slid one hand between my legs a second later, cupping my mound.

I squirmed and moaned and pleaded against his hand, howling to have my clit touched. Two of those big, rough fingers pushed into me and I came.

Rocking, bucking, screaming, I fucked his fingers as he thrust back. My vision blacked out and everything in my head became one long jagged pulse. The little pleasure nub in my brain shrieked happily, milking itself, forcing me to throw my hips into his wonderful hand.

As I jerked, he leaned down and bit one breast. It was the perfect bite.

Rough but tender. Wet, hot, and so fucking strong. He sank his teeth in hard enough to leave a mark, branding me as his.

I came harder, and his teeth never let go, not until my hips collapsed on the bed. His fingers peeled away, gently swirling inside my cunt, coating my clit in more wetness.

Growling, he shot me a *don't move a fucking muscle* look and sank beneath my waist. I wasn't even close to ready for him after coming so soon – or so I thought.

The few messy, stupid couplings I had with boys and the constant fears of rape had put me off real sex for a long time.

I didn't even know I could fuck and come again so soon until Maverick's tongue lashed through my labia. He licked me hard and slow, inhaling my scent and tasting me.

New heat instantly raged in my belly.

No, not heat. Hellfire.

My thighs closed around his shoulders. I felt him smile as he dug into me, pulling me open with his fingers to smother my clit with his tongue.

He licked. He sucked. He pinched his teeth lightly around my nub, corkscrewing pleasure so fast and hard through me I nearly passed out.

I was really fucking oxygen deprived now, but I didn't dare stop. Maverick carried me away, threw me to sky, and took absolute possession of everything I was with his mouth.

I came even harder the second time. My hands reached for his head, running my fingers through his thick hair, scratching at his neck.

He liked the encouragement. Maverick's tongue never missed a beat while I became a screaming, spasming mess beneath him.

When I could finally open my eyes, I stared at the ceiling, gasping for breath. I was flat on my back, and he'd gone from between my legs.

I forced my head up, careful not to let all the seething blood rush out at once.

Maverick stood at the end of the bed, wearing his sternest expression and nothing else. Naked.

"Holy shit!" I jerked up, hands behind me.

The alpha killer look on his face disappeared into a thin smile. The end of the mattress sank with his weight, and he crouched at the end of the bed, one hand fisted around his huge cock.

Clear pre-come dripped down his head to his fingers. It took me a full minute to process just how big he was – and not just the part between his legs.

Maverick was fucking huge. His whole massive chest was packed together like boulders and fully inked, covered in a flaming devil's head with fire shooting out around it. On both arms, his rugged biceps were covered with pitchforks, and big blocky letters scrawled next to those, giving him a wild kind of symmetry.

"YSBF?" I said, sounding out each letter.

"Your soul belongs forever." He pushed his arms out in front of him and flexed, giving me a better view. "Means we all sell our souls to this MC when we join. Forever, just like it says."

A chill went up my spine. In the fiery lust, I'd forgotten I was seriously bedding a man who belonged to the same kind of club that ruined my family and stole my youth.

The tattoos blazing on his skin reminded me no matter how sweet, strong, and handsome he seemed on the outside, deep inside he was a Prairie Devil. And not just a biker, but a President, a lifelong badass outlaw who was way past the point of no return.

For a split second, my brain tried to revolt, groping for reason. Then Maverick crawled toward me like a tiger, and pure desire chased reason and doubt back to their powerless holes.

"Fucking hell," he whispered, stopping when his body completely covered mine. "Forgot how damned perfect you looked laid out naked. Your shape, babe – fuck! Perfect hourglass."

I flushed. I always thought I could stand to lose a few pounds, but none of the men ever complained during my dances. Obviously, Maverick didn't either.

He lowered his head, breathing me in, raking the stubble on his chin across one breast. I shivered, wondering how many times my body could recharge and soar on wild desire.

Forever, maybe. As long as I'm with him...

"Do it, Maverick," I said, my voice trembling. I reached up and ran my hand over his cheek. "I need to feel you in me. Now."

"Babe, you don't have to ask."

He peeled back for a moment and reached next to me on the bed. I watched him tear a condom packet with his teeth, and then roll the rubber on his massive length.

"Soon as I claim you, I'm gonna get you set up to take it bareback. But for tonight, this'll have to do."

Bare. Just the idea sent cream trickling out helplessly between my thighs.

My pussy was beyond soaked. Something told me after we got through tonight, the whole damned bed would be stamped with our wet, potent lovemaking.

Maverick moved forward again. He rubbed the head of his huge cock up and down, up and down, teasing my opening until I rubbed my lips against him, crying out nonsensically.

The mewling noise I made pushed him over the edge. He grunted, pushed the sheets around my head with his fists, and thrust deep.

In one stroke, he was in me. I bit my lip and my eyes went wide as he tore into me. I might as well have been a virgin again as my sex struggled to take his fullness, huge and wide. He didn't stop until he edged my womb.

Then the real thrusting started.

Maverick's lips peeled back, baring his teeth as he fucked me.

Lovemaking? I wanted to laugh at what I'd thought earlier. *No, this is fucking, the very first time you're being really and truly fucked by a man.*

When I realized it, I bucked back with equal force. Wrapping my legs around his hard, muscular trunks was pure heaven. My surging excitement sent his primal urge to conquer, to mark, into overdrive.

Maverick thrust twice as hard, twice as fast. The old bed beneath us snapped and screamed, almost as loud as I gasped and moaned when he went balls deep.

I became a living, breathing furnace. The fireball that hadn't stopped burning in my lower belly since we'd gotten into bed exploded.

Raging, crackling, unstoppable fire surged up, devoured my brain, and then spread to all my extremities. I screamed, pinching him with my arms and legs as hard as I could.

Another orgasm – yes, *another!* – hit like lightning.

I came wet, came hard, taking the full body vibration of his flesh as he power fucked me.

Maverick grunted, forcing my legs apart with his hands when my climax tried to close them. He wrestled me against him, pulling me up around his cock with his hands.

The spasms were twice as hard as he sank deeper still. I couldn't believe how deep his fucking reached, straight to my soul.

Fire, flesh, and desire flashed stormed inside me. I wasn't sure where one climax ended and the next began. All I knew was an endless hurricane, spasms threatening to rip me apart forever.

"Fuck! So tight. So wet. So fucking sweet…brace yourself against me, baby, and don't you fucking stop grinding your hips. I'm gonna give you my come."

His come!

I forgot about the condom between us. My fevered brain thought he was serious, and thinking about the insane heat of his seed showered me in lust.

One more furious thrust and he held himself deep inside me, letting his cock swell.

The bestial part of my brain wanted him to explode inside me, to give me his essence, pure and hot and wonderful. I came like dynamite anyway when his cock bulged, firing his load into the condom, so hot I felt it even through the latex.

Sweating, screaming, rocking, my orgasm became his. The climax went on and on, enveloping us completely. I wanted it to last forever, to keep me close to the one man on earth I'd opened myself to.

"Oh, babe. Oh, my motherfucking cock…"

His soft words through sharp breaths woke me up. I felt him pull away from me slowly, stepping off the bed to dispose of the condom.

He returned and crashed next to me a minute later. I buried myself in his chest.

Why was his scent so stupidly intoxicating?

I breathed deep as he ran his fingers through my hair. I didn't say anything. No words seemed right to break the beautiful afterglow, and every stroke of his hand against my skin told me more than anything.

There was something special here. I'd tried to deny it, fight it, and fucking destroy it.

Now, safe in his arms and in his bed, I couldn't.

The June who'd come of age in hell, always on survival mode, drifted away. I felt her leave, as he jerked me to him, safe in his huge tattooed arms.

I didn't even wave goodbye. There was nothing about the last couple years remotely worth celebrating, and the ones before weren't so great either.

This, on the other hand, just might be the start of something better.

"Gotta tell you something, babe. Our secret," he whispered, when I was half-asleep. "I've only had two really amazing things in my life. You're number three. I'm old enough to know amazing is fucking rare, and it's something I never, ever let go of when it's right there in front of me. You're mine, June. Property of Maverick."

I moaned softly, too sleepy to give an adequate response.

The next morning, I woke to an empty bed and stretched. About what I expected. Maverick always got up before I did. Club business called, a bitch I'd have to share him with forever if this was really going anywhere.

It was the first time I'd woken up in years without a pounding headache, or soaked in last night's terror sweats. I rolled, pressed my face into his pillow, and filled my lungs with his scent.

God, I'd never stop loving that scent, no matter what the cards held for us.

One night changed everything. I know it sounds cliché and crazy.

I didn't believe it either until I was a solid week into my new role managing Pink Unlimited.

Maverick had given me more than a decent gig and some really mind blowing sex. He'd given me a second life.

I forced myself into the new role perfectly. Keeping my promise to him not to fuck up never seemed so easy.

I lived, breathed, and ate Pink Unlimited business for every waking hour. I hadn't even been around to thank my rugged benefactor, though he was just as scarce around the club that week due to some outside business.

I watched my reflection as I was backstage, arguing with Amber Lynn.

She was a local bitch with a sharp tongue and a double name. Maybe the dual names made her twice the bitch. Who knows?

"You're seriously telling me I can't offer a little tail on the back end? Girl, I've got guys coming out my ears who'd like more than a quick peek at what I'm offering."

"The club says no prostitution here," I said coldly.

Amber Lynn rolled her doe eyes. Bristling, I stepped forward, never taking my eyes off the long mirror behind her.

"Don't forget who's protecting your ass!" My hands shot out and I gave her a shove. "I wouldn't want to see what happens if you piss these guys off by bringing cops to sniff around here. Don't be greedy, bitch."

The stripper tottered backward on her high heels. For a second, I thought she'd fall and snap her neck, but she caught herself just in time.

"Jesus!" she spat, hands on her knees and looking sideways at me. "Okay! It's just that every other place I worked let me make some deals on the side, long as I gave them a cut…"

"This is not your old hooker job, Amber Lynn." I pointed toward the stage, where the burble of the audience behind the curtain was slowly rising. "You're here to shake your pretties and go home. Now, wipe the venom off your face and get out there. You're on."

She slunk away. I approached the mirror, proud of myself. I didn't want to treat my girls like dirt, but if they endangered this establishment or the MC protecting it, I had to let the bitch out.

And for once, letting her play hadn't blown up in my face.

I watched Amber Lynn around the bend backstage as she began her act. She was only a couple years older than me, a perky tanned girl who got the guys' attention.

Near the stage, a large figure in leather caught my eye. I stepped forward, peering through the darkness where the curtain separated.

"It can't be!" I blinked hard, trying to wipe the man's image away.

I prayed I was hallucinating, but God was not that kind. Underneath the stage stood Scoop, grinning up at Amber Lynn with his nasty beard and full Grizzlies colors on his jacket.

My chest tightened. Panic took hold, a thousand unsavory thoughts.

What if there were more of them here? What if they'd decided to strike just when Maverick took full security down a notch?

I ran, blowing right past the three girls lounging in their little rest areas.

"Miss Daniels?" Mandy called after me.

She was a sweet girl, and the one who caused the least mischief around here. I wasn't stopping, though – not when there was a chance these assholes could get at me when I thought I'd finally escaped them.

The big guy sat on a crate behind the bar. His Prairie Devils patched faced me, top and bottom rocker stretched tight as ever on his enormous shoulders.

"Tank!"

He turned, a cold beer in hand, and his dead pan expression brightened when he saw the terror in my eyes.

"Holy shit, what happened, June?" He was on his feet, towering over me.

"There's a guy wearing a Grizzlies cut by the stage...I recognize him. Don't know if he's come to scope the place out or if he's brought friends for something worse."

Tank spun, following my finger to the place where I pointed, straight through the crowd. His eyes narrowed like a hunter fixing on his prey.

"Fuck. He never should've slipped past the bouncers, unless he came in some other way. Gonna have to chat with those boys later." He turned back to me and gave my shoulders a reassuring slap with his giant paws. "Don't you worry. I got it."

"Just get him out of here," I said.

My voice was weak and small. Deadly hatred blazed to life in my brain, remembering how cruel the bastard by the stage looked while he raped Clara.

Something terrible was about to happen. Vulture didn't send his right hand man out to a rival business for no reason.

Even so, fear gave way to righteous anger. Tank was walking up to him now, pushing through the grinning, half-drunken men who were stuck on Amber Lynn's act.

I'd heard this guy was in the army before he joined the MC. I hoped he'd snap once the fight began, and break Scoop's brittle neck. Wouldn't be hard if the jackass gave him one little reason to.

Tank put his hand on Scoop's shoulder. The animal spun, and his eyes went wide when he saw three hundred pounds of pure muscle stuffed into a Prairie Devils jacket looking at him.

There were no words.

Tank's fist shot up, landing square on Scoop's jaw. The uppercut sent him flying through the air.

I almost jumped for joy when his body hit a table. Tank stood over him, cornering his target, hopefully warming up his sledgehammer fists for more.

People noticed the commotion. They screamed and began to stampede for the entrance. I flattened myself against the circular bar just in time to avoid getting run over. Up on the stage, Amber Lynn froze, covering her bare breasts and looking frantically around the room.

Shit! She needs to get the hell out of here.

I moved forward, carefully pushing past drunk guys flooding the opposite way. The air was thick with sweat, beer, and sex.

Stifling.

But I was confident. I kept on, until I was at the corner of the stage Amber had retreated to.

She looked down and saw me. Fear flickered in her eyes, and she huddled, shaking like a leaf.

Is this what I looked like when Maverick found me?

"Get back stage!" I shouted. "Tell the other girls to pack it in and head out. Shows are canceled tonight!"

She stared at me, then blinked. Finally, she spun and clicked her heels, her bare ass disappearing behind the bright pink curtain.

The tables around us were deserted. I exhaled relief when I saw there weren't throngs of crazed Grizzlies closing in on us.

"He's out. Won't finish the job unless Maverick gives the order." Tank's voice hummed with pride.

I moved past him, until I was staring at the face of the man who'd caused so much pain. He was laid out like he was asleep – the same blasted expression I'd seen a thousand times when he was passed out in the clubhouse after too much drinking.

My lungs buzzed. My heart pumped so hard blood roared in my ears, quieting the loud techno still throbbing in the speakers.

I reached to the floor and picked up a bottle. Tank cocked his head and gave me a weird look, but he wasn't moving.

Sick, deranged, rapist prick! Clara, my poor sister…this is for you.

I held the bottle's neck with both hands and smashed it down on the biker's forehead. Tank threw up his hands and grabbed me.

I fought him like a feral animal, screaming and crying and choking all at once.

Hot tears blurred my vision. Violent adrenaline rushed through me, swift and sharp. I thought I'd vomit all over the gorilla holding both my trembling wrists.

Glass shattering across his head woke Scoop up. He jerked his head, rolled off the table, and fell on the floor.

His disgusting body rolled more, twitching unnaturally. I wanted to spit on him while he was having a seizure. A concussion and the shakes wasn't half of what this piece of shit deserved for what he'd done.

Time seemed to fast forward. Other men were at our side, the bouncers the MC had hired to take care of day to day business.

"Get her out of here!" Tank snarled. "And as for this one…call a fucking ambulance. Got a feeling it's too early to haul this fuck out to a shallow grave in the mountains. Maverick's not gonna like this one bit."

I struggled with the bouncer too. I fought, spit, and hissed until he dragged me out into the cool night. The cool mountain air never failed to restore the senses, calming the most violent storms.

The volcanic eruption in my head boiled down to a simmer. I listened closely to the silent night, straining my ears.

Motorcycle engines roared in the distance, slowly closing in on Pink Unlimited's first disaster.

"He's out, brother. Just like I told you over the phone." Blaze spoke in a low, severe voice to Maverick as they stood over Scoop's mess on the floor.

"Shit!" Maverick spun and punched one of the tables hard, knocking it clean over. "This is the last fucking thing we need. This asshole in a coma, maybe worse…what the fuck am I supposed to say when the badge shows up to get everything on file?"

"Not a fucking clue. We were supposed to play it cool."

Blaze looked at me through the shadows separating us. His lip curled sourly and his brow furrowed.

He looked damn scary, and I had good reason to be nervous. He blamed me for breaking the Grizzlies goon's head.

Fuck you too, Mister Badass Biker. If only you knew what the man on the floor did to me, what he did to Clara…

"Cancel that ambulance," Maverick said to the bouncer standing near them.

"Have Shatter bring the truck around. We'll drop this fucknut off at the ER ourselves and beat it. The Grizzlies can pick him up, if he lives."

"You sure it's wise to leave a witness?" The doubt in Blaze's voice showed exactly what he thought about it.

Maverick stared him down. The dense air in the club turned prickly, electric, like a thunderstorm was going to start between the two.

"Don't question me on this. Not your fucking place, brother." Maverick stepped up, until he was in his face.

"We can't just dump him out in the woods. No fucking point when the idiot we hired phoned in an emergency and at least a hundred people here tonight saw everything go down. We fucking stomped him first."

"Shouldn't matter. He came into our strip club wearing enemy colors." Blaze pressed Scoop's side with his shoe.

"Oh, it fucking matters a lot, and you know it. If this sets off a war with the Grizzlies, we're gonna have a god damned Alamo situation at our clubhouse. I don't care how many new friends we've made in this little town. They've got the numbers as soon as they start calling up their guys from Seattle, Portland, Nor Cal, Nevada – "

Blaze held up his hands. "Fine. You've made your point, Aaron."

I pinched my eyes tighter, surprised to hear Maverick's brother call him by his real name.

"I don't need to do any convincing. I make the damned decisions here, Blaze. Don't like it, you can hit the fucking road. I won't even rat your pussy ass out to Throttle for abandoning ship."

They exchanged one more angry glare, and then Blaze turned sharply and stomped away. He went past me without so much as a second look.

I was expecting worse from him. I didn't think it would come from Maverick.

His men carried Scoop away to the truck outside while the MC President followed behind them. When they passed through the door, he stopped, avoiding my eyes.

"Tank. June. Get your asses backstage now."

He looked at the big guy first. I hadn't seen anything creepier for a long time than the burly veteran sulking past his President, cautious as ever, following his orders to a tee.

Then Maverick's wicked gaze turned on me, and I withered. There wasn't a trace of the love and lust we'd shared the other night, the night my body cried out to repeat many times over.

"Move it," he growled.

His voice was lower and fiercer than I'd ever heard it, warning me he wouldn't ask again, and definitely wouldn't take any sass. My heart dropped because it was missing *babe* too.

I shivered and moved.

Back-stage, I stood next to Tank, staring glumly at the floor. It hurt too much to look up at him just then, especially when I didn't know what the hell he wanted.

He stepped up to his MC brother first, enveloping the huge man in his dark aura.

"You were right to defend this club by throwing the first punch on our turf, brother."

"What?" Tank looked up, surprised. I was too.

Maverick moved like lightning, grabbing the open leather on his chest in both hands. Unbelievably, Tank shook, but I wasn't sure if it was from serious fear or the force of Maverick's hands.

"Let's talk about where you fucked up. I knew brains weren't your strong point since we picked your ass up in

Cassandra. Still, even a dumb fucker like you should know to ask a spy from a hostile MC what the fuck he was doing here!" Maverick's voice began like a growl and ended in a roar.

"I'm sorry, boss. I wasn't thinking – "

"Damned straight, you weren't!"

"It won't happen again. It's my training. I learned to neutralize threats in the service first. Wasn't ever an intelligence guy..."

"Bullshit excuses," Maverick spat.

He released Tank's cut and shook his head. The giant stood like an icicle. His face had gone red with anger, shame, or maybe both.

"One more fuck up like this and you *will* be having a special meeting with me and Throttle. Is that crystal fucking clear?" Maverick's eyes beamed through the darkness like a lion's.

"Perfectly clear, boss," Tank repeated. "I won't let you down again. I'll own up to my mistakes."

Maverick nodded. Satisfied.

"Do it, and get the hell out of my sight."

Tank shot me an apologetic look as he walked past. Maverick kept his back turned to me until we heard the door slam shut, and then he spun, making a direct line for me.

My heartbeat doubled. Sweat beaded on my forehead. I didn't want to take shit from this man, but I knew he had a shovel full for me, and there was no getting out of it.

Let's go. I'm not one of your MC buddies to boss around.

"You. What the hell were you thinking?" Pain swirled with anger in his voice. "The asshole you laid out on the floor was already down cold. Do you know what'll happen if that fucker ends up dead?"

"No," I lied.

I tried to be brave, but my voice slipped out in the faintest whisper. I knew damned well every MC defended its members like packs of wolves.

Whatever. I wasn't sorry. I didn't regret killing Scoop – if my bottle had actually destroyed his sick brain – not even a little bit.

"For a girl who's spent – what? – two years or more in the MC life, you don't know shit."

"More than that. My dad was in the Grizzlies."

Maverick's eyes narrowed. I hadn't breathed a word about my past before. I wasn't sure why I'd chosen now to reminisce, especially when the phrase motorcycle club was synonymous with nightmare.

"Damn it, June, my brothers and I are the *only* ones who give a shit about you. I'm trying to protect you from them and everybody else!" He licked his lips, skin steaming.

More than gross anxiety tightened up inside me. Damn, he looked hot like this. He was imposing, tinged with sweat, and his chest rose and fell in slow, shallow strokes.

Fuck me. I can't believe I'm getting wet for this asshole...

"Do you understand?" His eyes were big, pleading.

He grabbed me by the shoulders and pushed my face to his, so close I could feel his steaming breath. "I want you. Way more than I fucking should. But I'm not gonna let anybody put my club in danger – especially a woman who isn't any part of it."

Ouch. I pursed my lips, forcing myself to meet his wild eyed gaze.

"You're the one who doesn't understand!" The words exploded out of my mouth so harsh I had to stop for air. "You don't know shit about me. About him. I'm not gonna apologize for bashing his head in, Maverick. I'm not sorry, and I'd do it again in a heartbeat."

He moved, lifting his head up to his full height, towering over me. Maverick looked at me like something he'd eat for lunch.

I squirmed and gasped as his hands shot around my back. He pulled me toward him, tugging me so hard I started to climb his chest to breathe, my feet dangling on the ground.

We were at eye level again, but it was *his* level. He was telling me he wouldn't lower himself to mine if I didn't cooperate.

"Then you better start talking, baby." His hands squeezed my ass, angry and rough. "Because if you don't have a damned good reason for putting my MC in serious danger, your ass is gone, no matter how much Pink and my cock will miss you."

"Fuck you!" I screamed. "They fucking raped my sister!"

I clapped my lips shut. The words echoed through the emptiness like a lone bullet being discharged.

Maverick's grip softened. His eyes were big and clear, *shocked*. I never imagined that look before.

"What? When?"

"Years ago. Right after they killed my dad and shot up my junkie Mom...the asshole who came in here tonight and the bigger asshole over him. Their VP, Vulture. They kept us as slaves. I tried to keep Clara together, tried to get us free...but I fucked up. I got her raped and she broke. Found her dead the next morning with a bunch of fucking empty pill cartons in her lap."

Maverick sat me on the floor, but kept his arms around me. He looked like he'd been smacked in the forehead.

"Jesus Christ," he whispered.

I was weeping all over his huge arms at this point, spilling my tears on his tattoos. All at once, he threw himself around me, embracing me with everything he had.

I blubbered like a baby for the next five minutes. Monsters rattling their cages for far too long frolicked free in my head.

I saw my father's dead, beaten face smeared in his own blood. Then Clara's chalk white expression as she lay limp and cold in my arms, her eyes sunken back in her head from the poison she'd taken.

"You can help me," I whispered, as soon as I could speak. "Help me get the one thing that'll finally make me whole, Maverick. Please."

Tight, angry wrinkles lined his face when he looked at me. "I can't feed your need for vengeance openly with my club as Maverick, President of the MC."

My heart sank and I started crying harder again. Only for a second.

"Unofficially, as Aaron Sturm, it's another story. After what you just said, I couldn't live with myself if I didn't work out some way to destroy the fucking animals who've caused you so much pain." He leaned into me, pouring vicious heat into my ear. I whimpered in his arms.

"Don't breathe a word about this to anybody else, babe. I won't let it go. Not until they break, bleed, and die at your feet. I promise."

VI: Acrobatics (Maverick)

"Jesus! Maverick! You're fucking killing me!"

The bed rocked maniacally beneath us as I drove into her. I had June beneath me, on her hands and knees, sweet ass bobbing as I slammed myself into her for all I was worth.

I reached around her front side and grabbed her tits.

Her buds felt fucking amazing between my fingers. I pinched them, reminding her who was in control, and she loved every nasty second. Her sweet cunt got ten degrees hotter, wetter, opening deeper for me.

It was the first time fucking her bare, and I was going to claim her with all nature's fury. The pill protected her from anything crazy happening, but my cock didn't know that.

Thrusting into her, nothing mattered except shooting seed up her womb. I swore I'd fill her belly up and leave her leaking my essence for a good long time.

I yanked her hair, forced her lower, pulling her ass up to meet my thrusts.

Harder, deeper, better...

June arched her back and came for the second time, swiveling her hips against me, grinding and milking my cock. I jackhammered in for the send off, fucking through her climax.

With this woman, nothing would ever be easy or soft. She needed to break, to feel, to surrender wrapped around my thickness, all for her own fucking good.

"Fuck, babe! Your heat – "

I couldn't say another word. I rammed forward and exploded, reigniting her climax, prolonging an orgasm tearing through her so hot and intense she gasped for precious oxygen.

I forgot to breathe too. But fuck it, my lungs didn't need to work when I was balls deep inside her, emptying myself, shooting my come straight up her hot little womb.

My cock jerked, spitting its searing load again and again. Nobody made me come like June.

I'd fucked my share of whores and small town sluts, many of them tens. They had the tits and ass, but they didn't turn every fucking muscle in my body to stone like June, not like the girl – the only girl – I ever called "babe."

My heart pumped, sending badly needed blood to my bulging muscles. The rest of me just kept coming, rippling with raw heat, burning up in her sweet, endless inferno. Fuck, she'd be the death of me if I wasn't careful.

My body, mind, and soul only cared about hurling my seed into her as deep as I could.

I wanted to mark her as mine. Like, really fucking mark her, inside and out.

Soon she'd be branded with more than just my seed. Wouldn't be long until I took her as an old lady, and then she'd get the tattoo showing everybody she was my property.

Until then, I'd make do by fucking her, coming in her, licking and sucking every inch that belonged to me.

And, of course, keeping her safe from everything, including her fucked up past.

We sighed together as she collapsed beneath me. I pulled away, though I could've went on drilling her. With June, my cock never went completely limp. It was always ready and never fully spent, not when I wanted to give her everything in my soul.

I flopped down next to her, enjoying the rest. It was our second fuck of the morning since I'd gotten up before dawn with a bad case of wood, and our first time together since she told me she'd taken the pill long enough to give condoms the finger.

Shit. You're only a heartbeat away from sharing her bed every night, buddy.

Fucking shit. How will I ever sleep again?

"I'm glad things are simple in bed," she murmured, reaching up to stroke my brow. "We lay down. We fuck. We let the fire take away everything else."

I grinned. "Best kinda therapy there is, babe."

June laughed a couple times. Hearing her laugh was as beautiful as the little mountain birds out here who came down from nowhere to sing in the springtime mornings, and almost as rare.

Not that I shared that with anybody.

Nobody wearing the patch was gonna get all deep and flowery about nature. But I wasn't gonna pretend I didn't appreciate it.

My ears prickled happily. If she was satisfied, then so was I.

"Therapy…I always used to worry about getting my sister a shrink whenever I thought about running away from them…guess I hadn't given it any thought for myself." Familiar sadness clouded her eyes.

I flattened my hands on her back, pulling her to my chest. No fucking way was I gonna let her get too far along with that talk again.

Wasn't good for her. Besides, my cock was starting to regain feeling again, and it would be hard and hungry in another second.

"Don't worry about it. Seriously." I looked her right in the eye. "You're doing just fine here, getting your shit together. What went down at the strip club the other night was just a fucking bump in the road. Learn from it."

"If somebody with a broken brain like me can learn anything. I'm tired of making mistakes." She lowered her face, resting just beneath my chin, inhaling my scent.

Mischievous. If she thought I was gonna let her off that easy, she had another thing coming.

"You keep saying that, and it's wrong," I said, firmly tilting her chin until she faced me. "It's bullshit. I don't give half a fuck how crazy or damaged you say you are. You're mine now, and I'm gonna iron out every last one of your kinks. Stop doubting yourself and you'll find out just how smooth you can be."

That got her attention. June raised her head and I kissed her, seizing her mouth the same way I cupped her ass, like I belonged there.

My hand brushed her pussy. Just as I expected, she was getting wet, dripping cream and the last load I'd blown in her.

Fuck. Wet and wild and still absolutely fucking hot.

My finger pushed in, ready to warm her up. Then a fist banged on the door and I jerked up.

"This better be life or fucking death," I said.

I edged past her and threw my legs over the bed. Didn't even bother throwing on pants – if it was some bullshit, it could wait for me to finish with her.

The doorknob practically ripped off in my hands. Shatter was on the other side, and I knew it was serious. Any other time he would've busted out laughing when I greeted him buck naked with a wet and ready girl in my bed.

"We need everybody out here, Prez. Several bikes just pulled up at the clubhouse and there's more on the way. Not ours. Grizzlies."

"Fuck!" I slammed the door in his face and went for my jeans.

June got up. She threw off the blanket covering her and was at my side, yelling in my ear.

"Stay with me!" she begged. "I don't want to deal with them alone…not again."

The terror in her eyes was real, but I had to keep moving. Pushing her away tugged on my heart, but the club came first. Hell, if this place went down, June wouldn't be safe anyway.

It was up to me to defend my castle, my men, and my woman.

I jerked on my jeans and zipped up without looking for my boxers. Threw on my shirt and leather cut, all the while pushing her away.

"Sit down and stay quiet, babe. My boys need me. I won't let these fuckers anywhere near you. They won't get that far."

The door flew open with a jerk and I slammed it behind me. Everybody else was already lined up by the main entrance.

Blaze looked at me, annoyed. If it wasn't so dire, I would've punched him in the ribs to wipe the look off his face. Still, dealing with the Grizzlies was a lot more important than bickering with my fucking half-brother just now.

"Everybody armed?" I asked.

All four of my brothers nodded.

"How many?"

"Ten bikes, and at least that many more circling our stretch of road. Fuckers just showed up outta nowhere. Tank saw them pull in and ran inside to get me."

Fuck. Five guys against two dozen or more. I wasn't afraid to do serious battle. Just hated the way the odds were starting out stacked against us.

"Brought you an extra, boss." Tank reached toward me and I grabbed the gun out of his hand.

Everybody else had theirs drawn too, with Hypno behind us holding a high powered shotgun. Better than nothing, but we needed full auto for this.

With their numbers, the Grizzlies were likely to break through all our entrances, swarming us in every direction.

An engine revved. I watched a Harley pull up with the roaring bear painted on its casing.

A tall man with a disheveled beard and nasty long hair climbed off. He motioned to his other guys to stay back while he walked to our door.

"Come on out, Devils! Just wanna have a neighborly talk since you took a steaming shit all over our truce."

Bullshit.

I waited. The evil morning stillness hung thick, so silent I heard all my guys breathing.

"Don't make me fucking ask again!" He slapped the glass hard with his fist. "I wanna talk to Maverick. Man to man. We can do it the easy way or I'll light your fucking club on fire."

Smiling, he stepped aside, waving to his men. My nerves blazed when I saw he meant what he said literally.

Several guys across the lot held up huge red drums of gas, grinning like idiots.

The Grizzlies were just crazy enough to do it too. They were infamous for blowing up rival warehouses in their war with the cartels further south.

"We could drag him inside," Blaze said. "I saw the VP patch on the fucker's jacket. A hostage officer just might do us some good."

"No." I stood tall, no longer crouching with my gun, making the last few steps to the door. "Let me go. By the time we haul his ass in here, the place could burning or under heavy fire. I'm sure they're packing more than gasoline cans. Look out the windows over there if you don't believe me."

I motioned. Everybody's eyes flicked in the right direction, and they saw the other five bikes parked there, their riders dismounted and creeping up to our fire exit.

"Bastard's got us by the balls. I'll talk to him."

I didn't look at my guys as I pulled the door open. The VP looked even nastier up close. His leathery skin reeked of tobacco.

"If you're really here to talk, then come in." He gave me a nasty smile and I flashed my gun. "But if you move a single step in our clubhouse past my men, or give any kind of signal, we're letting bullets do the speaking instead."

He shrugged. "Your funeral."

I took several steps back, never once taking my finger off the trigger. He followed me, and I signaled for my boys to give us some space.

"All clear," he said sharply, turning his mouth to the radio in his breast pocket. Then he looked at me. "You know what this is about, Maverick."

He knew my name. And I knew his. Vulture, VP of the Missoula Grizzlies, the monstrosity on two legs who'd taken my girl's soul.

"Do I?" I wasn't going to give him anything and make him think he was justified.

"Yeah. You Prairie fucks have overstayed your welcome. As VP of the Missoula Grizzlies, I don't appreciate one of your assholes sending a broken bottle across my brother's head!" He was practically screaming. "You fucked up, asshole. *You* fucking trashed our agreement, and I don't do seconds."

I didn't even flinch. I'd had bigger guys than him yelling in my face since I was old enough to jerk off, and the only thing bad about this fuck stain was his breath. It was easy to forget he had thirty guns trained on us, ready to blast clean through our doors and windows.

Play it cool. Give the asshole what he wants. There's plenty of time to take it back later.

He was bullshitting. Flexing.

The only notice most MCs give when war breaks out is a bomb in a shipment or a few dead men with the rival club's letters carved in their chests. If the asshole in front of me wanted war, we would've had it by now.

This wasn't a declaration of war. This was a negotiation.

"That was an accident. Don't play innocent with me, VP." I sneered at his title. "I'm guessing you're like me. Been in this business a long time. We both know damned well you don't send a patched in member to another club's titty bar just for fun."

"I'm not a fucking retard. I know what you're accusing. Still doesn't excuse beating my man to pieces. Especially when *you're* the fucking guests in these borderlands, a long ways from home." He reached out and pushed one finger into my chest.

I caught his filthy wrist and twisted it backward. Would've been lovely to keep bending until it snapped, but I wasn't ready to go kamikaze yet. I let him go before I did any serious damage, and he jerked his hand away.

"Listen to me, asshole. You've got more chips on the table than I do, but I've got plenty too, or else there wouldn't be a game at all," I said. "I know what you want: restitution for putting one of your guys in the ICU."

Vulture looked at me, frowning and admitting nothing. Finally, he stepped closer. I felt every guy behind me tighten fingers on their guns.

"Blood for blood," he said coldly.

"Fuck off. We both know this game's really played with money. Wouldn't be any blood between MCs at all if it weren't for dollars – "

"Dollars *and* reputations," he corrected.

I glared. "I'll give you a twenty percent cut of Pink Unlimited's profits for the next year if you back the fuck off and drag your ass back to Missoula."

"Thirty percent."

I cocked my head. "Fine. We both know this is stopping at twenty five, but I'll need to take five off the top to cover the backend so the IRS doesn't get suspicious."

"IRS," he hissed. "Whatever. You pussy boys want to play by the rules, go ahead. You'll be lucky to keep this place in booze and women with the way I'm skinning you."

He extended his hand. I didn't hold his greasy fucking palm a second longer than I needed.

Dumbass. Easiest deal I never had to negotiate.

I was laughing in my head, but I didn't show a single tooth outwardly. With one more death glare, he was about to turn, when something behind me caught his eye. Vulture circled past me.

"Hey! Where the fuck do you think you're going?"

Fuck. He'd crossed the line and then some, moving past my boys. Everybody had their guns raised and trained on him, and I could practically hear the rifles and handguns going up behind the windows and doors.

Then I saw what he was after.

June.

She stood just at the end of the long hall where the bar led to our rooms. Vulture walked up to her like he owned the place.

"My, my. Been a long fucking time since I seen that pretty face, darlin'. Forgot they took you as collateral.

Better you than that sweet pussycat sister of yours, I suppose. What was her name?"

The room went deadly silent. Blaze looked at me, waiting for the least little signal to fire.

I looked to the side, out the window near the Fire Exit. Fifteen guys had their guns perfectly fixed on us, ready to shatter the glass and fill us with screaming lead the second we hit their boss.

Motherfucking Mexican standoff.

We're fucked. Screwed, blued, and tattooed.

We were boned in every way. But I was ready to hit self-destruct if he didn't take his nasty hand off her face right fucking now.

June screamed. She lunged, clawing at his neck. He slapped her across the face, and I exploded.

I charged, blowing past my guys. I know somebody would've fired if I wasn't in the fucking way.

I knocked him flat on the floor, and then whipped out my pistol. I didn't fire, but I brought it down on his head again and again.

"Fuck!" Two guys screamed at the same time as a window blew in.

Shrapnel exploded around us, but the firing stopped after one volley. Everything was eerily silent again, except for my own heavy breathing plus June's whimpers.

Beneath me, the asshole coughed. Vulture squirmed, and I reluctantly took my knee off his back.

Laughing, he stood and wiped the blood from his lip.

"Hold your fire," he growled into his radio.

"Hey, man, I just wanted to admire something that used to belong to me. Nothing personal." He took several steps past me, staggering toward the door. "Don't worry. I won't take the fat bitch away from you. Don't need to have her back when I've left my mark on her forever."

I swallowed. Hard. Foamy spit rushed down my dry throat, one movement away from going mad dog.

Vulture was gone. Too many engines to count revved at once. They left us in our mess, surrounded the deafening Harley roar.

I looked around. There was blood on the floor, and not all of it Vulture's. One of the glass fragments had grazed Tank near the temple, and steady blood caked the side of his face.

He looked at me and grinned. I nodded, and relaxed as soon as I saw none of my guys were hurt.

I went to June, grabbed her, and held her tighter than ever before. She broke, weeping into my leather. I stroked her hair, finally able to hear my own savage heartbeat now that the enemy bikes were gone.

"Have a little patience. A little faith. They haven't taken shit." I cleared my throat, and my next words were louder. "As I stand here, with God and my brothers as witnesses, I will kill them. Every last member of the Missoula Grizzlies has a painful death on the way by these hands, and there's no fucking stopping it."

I'd been through tense church meetings in my time, but nothing as bad as this.

The room was dead quiet. So damned eerie silent we heard our local supporters sweeping up the busted glass and repairing the window outside our little meeting room.

We were all gathered at the table. I looked at my brothers' faces one by one, staring into shell shock and blinding rage.

Blaze sat tall in his chair, across from me at the other end, holding his fists on the wood beneath him like a statue.

Whatever was on his mind, it was fucking intense. And I wanted it dealt with first, before he spread his dark energy through the MC like always.

"Looks like you've got something to say, brother." I mustered the coolest voice I could. "Don't hold it in. Bad juju can hurt a man, you know."

"Yeah, I do. I think your brain's gone to your ass, Maverick." All eyes turned to him.

"Your little promise out there to kill the Grizzlies…was that a fucking joke? Ever since this stray pussy showed up as collateral, you've been too busy petting her and putting the club at risk. Every week we're getting further and further away from what we we're supposed to be doing out here. That means mother charter's gonna keep us here longer. Fuck, will we ever be Nomads again?"

"That's bullshit, and you know it. There's more to being a Nomad than riding across state lines and wearing the patch. We're not anchored to any charter, true, but we serve the MC. We're here to take care of business and get the fuck out."

He shook his head. "You sure that's what we're really here for?"

I stared him down, waiting to see if he was finished, or if my brother was gonna go all the way. He stopped just short of calling for a vote on my leadership.

Doubted the fucker had the balls.

"We came out West to muscle into new territory and net the whole MC some nice money. Everybody wearing the new Python patch knew the risks. Guess what?" I folded my hands and leaned forward. "Those risk are now realities, brothers. I don't give a shit how big and bad the Grizzlies are, or how many bears they can wrangle from the coast. We're Prairie Devils, and Devils don't let themselves get shoved around by anybody. What happened out there was a fucking disgrace, and we won't let it go."

The same deadly silence lingered in the room. I had their full attention, including Blaze's.

"YSBF." I pulled up my shirt and tapped my bicep where the phrase was scrawled, reminding everybody who had the same tattoo what it really meant. "Your Soul Belongs Forever. If that's not true for anybody here, then you can turn in your patches and get the fuck out."

Shatter and Hypno shared a quick, uneasy glance. Blaze and Tank were looking right at me. They accepted my challenge with firm nods.

"Just for the record, you're dead fucking wrong, brother." I looked straight at Blaze, my brother in blood, steel, and leather. "Hitting the Grizzlies isn't about pussy. It's about this club's reputation."

"Then the deal's a double-cross?" Tank asked quietly.

"Damned right it was. They fucked us over by sending their guy over to our strip club in the first place. We don't honor truces with fucks who don't honor ours. They aren't getting shit from Pink Unlimited or any other business under our protection."

The other guys nodded more vigorously. Even Blaze looked satisfied. He had his reasons to distrust me – plenty – but he was the same as me at heart.

He didn't believe in taking shit from anyone. His fists, knives, and guns were always ready for a fight, no matter how uneven the odds.

The Prairie Devils were an old club, formed on the plains in blood and fire. Nobody who wore the patch honorably was afraid of dying for this MC. If I had to choose tarnishing myself like a chickenshit coward or being torn apart by five hundred Grizzlies, I'd choose the latter any day in a second.

"If we're gonna take them on, then we need more support than this. Backup." Blaze tapped the table, knocking the big rings around his fingers on wood loudly.

"I'm making the call to Cassandra tomorrow. Throttle won't like it, but he won't let us get torn to pieces out here. He'll send reinforcements from his charter or the Dickinson group half a state over, our closest brothers."

"What about weapons? The shit we're armed with isn't gonna cut it. Did you see what those fucks were packing today?" Shatter brushed his lips with anxious fingers. He was jonesing for a cigarette, and talking out logistics about some very serious shit didn't help soothe his nerves.

"You're right. We're gonna need a lot more from mother charter. We can't match the Grizzlies in numbers, but firepower's another story," I said.

"Trouble is, you can't use it and get away with it. The minute machine guns and RPGs start going off in a little town like this – or hell, up in Missoula – the Feds will land on us and break our fucking necks." Once again, Blaze was both a cynical asshole and the voice of reason.

"We'll figure it out. One thing's for sure: their numbers have made them sloppy over the years. The Grizzlies are used to throwing their fucking weight around. They don't do much planning. That's why the cartels are kicking their asses down in Cali."

No response. I hadn't figured out the nitty-gritty yet, but I was going to.

I waited another minute in silence. When nobody else popped up with questions, comments, or smart ass remarks, I slammed both fists on the table.

"Church adjourned. Now, go out there and help get this place back in order. We're gonna keep to ourselves and stay the fuck away from the Grizzlies while we wait for our support. And then we'll hit those fucks so hard we blow their hair back. Understood?"

"You got it, Prez," Hypno said, speaking for everybody.

"Fucking outrageous, Maverick! You weren't supposed to engage those assholes unless it was completely necessary." Throttle shouted so loud his voice distorted through my phone.

"That's what you're not getting, brother. It absolutely fucking was." I shook the shitty burner phone once.

Silence.

"They were definitely scoping us out. Probably looking for weak points, girls to take hostage, or just shit to stir up and give our new strip club a bad name. My guy fucked up bashing heads before pumping our guest for info. But cracking his skull was totally justified, and you know it."

Another pause, and then Throttle spoke, this time more calmly. "I don't know shit about what's going on out there. Fuck up or not, I'm not gonna let a whole charter get massacred on my watch."

"Then you're cool with the backup?"

"I didn't say that. I said I'd send men and guns out there, yeah, but I'm definitely not fucking cool until I see what's going on myself. You can expect us on Friday. Be ready."

"Throttle?" I shook the phone again, hoping the disposable POS hadn't dropped the call.

It had ended, almost certainly on his terms. Whatever, the dead tone in his voice told me all I needed to know.

Fuck. I wanted help from mother charter, not the head honcho looking over my shoulder.

Everything has a fucking price.

I closed the phone and threw it on my little desk. I reached for the folder in front of me, kicked back in my chair, and paged through the stack.

The numbers from Pink Unlimited's first couple weeks were looking good.

This county had been too damned dry on pussy and fun for a long time. Even the fight with the Grizzlies hadn't stopped people from returning.

I ran my finger down one page carefully, doing numbers in my head. It all added up perfectly. Told me June hadn't lost focus and started any bad habits. She signed off on the papers shortly after she'd been threatened and touched by the piece of shit who visited our club.

Thinking about Vulture made me want to snap his scrawny neck with my bare hands. I still hadn't seen her since the standoff.

That was going to change tonight. I wouldn't talk club business with her or make promises I couldn't keep.

But I intended to make damned sure she knew I had her back, her heart, her sweet body, and I wasn't gonna fucking let it go for anything.

I walked out of my cramped office near midnight and slammed the door. Walked past Hypno, Shatter, and Tank defusing from a long day with whiskey at the bar. Blaze was in a booth near the back with some brunette from town, sliding his hand up her thigh and cooing in her ear.

I fought the urge to walk over and ask why he wasn't out scouting supply routes for the new drug runs like he promised, but I wasn't in the mood for a bullshit story.

No matter what came out of his mouth, the real reason was on his lap, tipsy and giggly as ever.

Fucking hypocrite. And he has the balls to get on my ass about shrugging duty over pussy…

Throwing myself on my bike, I revved up the engine and grabbed the handlebars.

The rumble of my Harley's engine had always been a comfort. Its sweet, one of a kind music never failed to tame the beast within, no matter how rabid.

Nothing but raw power wedged between a man's legs. Merciless, non-judgmental, and a warning to any weaker boys that they better stay out of your fucking way.

I roared down the cool mountain roads toward Python.

Ten minutes later, I went in through the strip club's backdoor. Behind the curtain, the show was on, with two or three girls shaking their moneymakers to jeering crowds.

June sat by herself at a little desk she'd set up in her old cubicle. I smiled, happier than ever I'd taken her pretty ass off the dance floor.

It was painful enough seeing other guys eating up her body with their hungry eyes when I barely knew her. Now?

I'd fucking put anyone else who saw her naked through the roof, and then stuff their balls down their throat.

"You've stayed out plenty long tonight, babe." I settled a stiff hand on her shoulder, gently massaging her. "Tip sheets and receipts can wait 'til morning."

She looked up, and I saw surprise mingling with the usual sadness in her eyes.

Fuck, not again. Just when I'd been making some progress washing the darkness from her soul, the fuck who got close to her had brought it back, slapping a new coat of melancholy over my hard work.

"I really should finish these up, Maverick…"

"It's Aaron tonight."

She blinked and pursed her lips. Didn't blame her one bit.

That's right, babe. Tonight's about me and you. Fuck the club business, and running this place too.

"What the hell's gotten into you?" she whispered, glancing around anxiously. Probably didn't want the two girls a few feet away dolling themselves up for the next show to overhear.

"This."

I wasn't playing around anymore. I swooped low, picking her up. Her little hands slapped playfully on my back, and then I had her in my arms, hauling her out to my bike.

The strippers laughed as we walked past. I shot them a look to keep their ruby red lips shut, and they complied.

Funny irony, I thought, carrying June out the back entrance. *I've seen that look in a woman's eyes a thousand times.*

Fear. Jealousy. Obedience.

She doesn't realize she fascinates me because I can't read her. June Daniels is a big fucking mystery for me to crack, and I'm gonna rock her until something breaks open.

She wasn't fighting me anymore as I settled her on my bike. It was a cold night, even with the spring days getting longer.

I helped her bind her hands around my waist and we took off. The ride was like a sweet repeat of the first one I'd given her on these dark roads, the night I'd put an end to her defiance and turned her into a lover – my lover, my woman.

That's one re-run I wasn't fucking tired of watching – and feeling. Having her hands and thighs coiled snug around me was a special pleasure I wouldn't ever get sick of.

She didn't just ride bitch on my bike's backseat. She rode with me, more like an equal because she knew how to stand her ground.

Mine.

If I wanted a whore to throw herself at me, I could've found at least ten back at the strip club. Right now, the only woman I'd ever want was pressed tight on my bike as we rocketed down the road, and nothing was gonna change that.

Not the Grizzlies. Not my MC. Not even her.

"What is it, babe? Talk to me." I stroked the side of her face.

We lay in my bed, my cock straining in my jeans as I spooned her plump ass. Took a lot to ignore the greedy bastard, but I knew something wasn't right.

"Him."

I bit down, grinding my jaw. We both knew who she was talking about – a ruthless asshole who didn't deserve to occupy a single cell in her brain.

"Fuck *him*," I repeated, venom in my voice. "Give me a few more weeks. If Vulture and his men aren't deep in their graves by summer, then I'll be there myself."

She turned, worry lining her eyes. "That's what I'm afraid of. This seems reckless. I can't ask you to put yourself in danger – let alone the whole club – all because of what happened to me."

"You're not. The bastards in Missoula need to go for more reasons than your personal vengeance." I lowered my face, nuzzling hers with my stubble and breathing her sweet scent.

Fuck, she smelled good. Like lilac or lavender, if those things made a person horny as hell instead of putting them to sleep.

"You can't just go charging in, Aaron," she said sharply. I stiffened when she used my real name. "Please. They're brutal. They won't take any prisoners. I don't think I'll be able to live with myself if I get more people killed."

"You won't. Love you, babe, but I'm not talking club business. All I can tell you is the only people dying are gonna be Grizzlies. Well deserved too."

I squeezed her. She turned away, tears and rage brimming in her eyes.

Damn it, this wasn't the way I wanted things tonight. The more we talked about the fucks up north, the more it brought her bad memories, pulling them down like a dark curtain.

Pushing one hand through her hair, I brought it down her shoulders, drawing my fingertips across her soft skin. She shivered.

"I want you to get one thing straight: I'm claiming you, June. When a member of this MC takes an old lady, it means she's part of this club, the same as my brothers and I. If anyone fucks with her, they fuck with us. If they think they can get away fucking with a club asset and a President's old lady, then they better hope they're right with God because there's no going back. None."

"I don't know." Her words were full of doubt, but hope rang in her voice.

I kissed her. Hard. Claiming her sweet mouth, tasting her warmth, her essence.

"I don't know the first thing about being an old lady...it's scary," she said.

"Bullshit." I smiled as she blinked in surprise. "You've been through hell, June, and maybe that's why I've decided you're fucking perfect for me. You're not afraid of this life. Not afraid of me."

I squeezed her thigh, rounding to her plush ass with the same pressure. She jerked against me, gasping, her skin's temperature rising.

"That's right, babe. Let me feel that fucking fire. Give it all to me, and I'll keep it safe. Won't let it flame out."

She kissed me back this time. My tongue went wild, instantly plunging into her mouth, claiming her tongue and stroking the warm velvet behind her lips.

I kissed the way I intended to fuck her. My cock twitched, angry and ready.

My hands drew off her and started to fiddle with my jeans. But I stopped, glancing down when I felt her little hands on mine.

"Let me," she whispered, breaking the kiss.

I lay flat on the bed, almost in disbelief as she got up and crawled toward my lap. Everything beneath my waist turned to pure fire when she popped my button, undid my zipper, and yanked my jeans down.

A second later, my cock was in her hand, hard and dripping pre-come on her skin. She shot me a look with narrowed eyes and pursed lips, the kind of look a whore hones to perfection.

But no stripper, whore, or biker bitch I'd ever fucked looked at me with love in their eyes too.

She rolled my seething tip in her fingers, spreading the pearly slickness down my length. Her fingers wrapped around my shaft and squeezed, and I jerked as my balls instantly puckered.

Fuck.

"Fuck!"

I thought it. I said it. I even fucking felt it right down to my very being as she lowered her sweet lips and took me into her mouth.

I'd been waiting to have her mouth on my cock for weeks. Now, I'd gotten my filthy wish, but I never imagined in a million years she'd suck and lick like she did.

June's lips tightened over my skin. She sucked me deep, forcing herself as low as she could go, cupping my balls with one palm and giving them a gentle pressure that only added to my wicked fire.

She looked right at me when she sank down again, burying me in her slick, beautiful warmth. My hand went for her head. I laced my fingers through her hair and sighed fucking deep.

"God damn! Where'd you learn to suck cock like that, babe?" Her tongue flicked up around my crown and I almost unloaded in her mouth. "Fuck me! I don't give a shit. Just. Keep. Doing it."

She took orders like a champ. Her tongue darted around me again and again, toying with my flesh, but also worshiping it.

My balls tightened up in her hand, getting ready to blow. June sucked like she sensed it coming, making her strokes shallower, hotter, wetter, and tonguing me in the same irresistible place.

Fuck! That one nasty word echoed in my head a dozen times.

My hips bucked at her mouth, making the bed rock beneath us. My eyes were nearly pinched shut when she shot me another big, doe-eyed plea with her bright eyes.

Do it.

And I did. I let go, grunting like a beast as seed ripped up my shaft, exploding at the tip in blinding hot jets shot past her lips.

I filled her pretty mouth with my come, growling and thrusting along her tongue the whole time. She didn't even flinch as she loosened up and swallowed it all.

A small trickle escaped the corner of her mouth and spilled back onto me. I watched in awe as my spasms waned. She dove, licking up my shaft, cleaning my cock like a total addict.

"Come here," I growled, yanking her tight to my chest when my boner went soft.

"I'm gonna repeat myself. Where'd you learn to do that?"

She shrugged and smiled mysteriously. "Yours is only the third one I've sucked in my life. Guess when you're around whores and strippers for years, you see and hear a lot of things."

I gave her a quick smack on the ass. She jumped.

Feeling her tits smashed against my chest was getting me hard again already.

"That's for keeping secrets. Even good ones. You're gonna tell me everything when you're my old lady. The good, the bad, the ugly, and yeah – the sexy too."

My hand was slowly traveling down her curves as I spoke. I pushed my fingers down her pants and cupped her mound, giving it a good squeeze.

Shit, she was wet, swollen, and hot.

All for me. My cock stiffened between us like it hadn't shot off at all tonight.

"You mean I don't get any privacy?" she asked me with a smile, but I knew she was halfway serious.

"Only in your own head, babe. Trust me – it's gonna be a bear for me too. I've spent my whole life on the outskirts, building fences to keep things safe from my brothers, my enemies, my own brother and sister…"

"Sister? You've never mentioned one before."

I hadn't called Aimee for more than a month. Not since I got out West, into the eye of the storm. Long as she was off the shit that had nearly fucked her over in our dusty little hometown, everything was cool.

"Half sister to Blaze and I, really. You'll meet her someday." Crazy alarms rang in my head. I hadn't ever thought about introducing a girl to my family. "There. One less secret on my end."

She smiled. "I'm starting to like this game."

"No game, June. Seeing how fast and hard you can ride my cock, on the other hand…"

She squealed and laughed as I held her down. My fingers pushed inside her. I fingered her fast and hard until neither of us could take it anymore.

Then I helped her to straddle me. She worked off her top and bra as I went for her pants. Practically tore the lacy new knickers she'd bought to shreds in my crazy fucking haste.

My cock stood up like a rail. I grunted, feeling steam pouring off my skin as she opened, carefully lowering herself onto the thick pillar jutting out between my legs.

Enveloped in her wetness, I went wild.

We fucked hard, gradually upping our rhythm, kindling fire between us. I reached up, grabbed her breasts, stroking her nipples soft between my fingers.

June looked sexy as hell when she threw her head back. The room was a little stuffy with the volatile springtime air. I watched beads of sweat roll down her tits and onto her stomach, wishing I could bend and trail each one with my tongue.

There'd be plenty of time for that later. Right now, I wanted my baby girl to come her brains out rocking on me while I filled her empty heat with mine.

She moaned a little louder each time she fucked, breathing and rolling her eyes. But I sensed her holding back, still drifting on shitty thoughts.

My hands found her ass. I held her against me, the better to thrust up into her. One palm darted out and smacked her.

June squealed and looked at me. "Harder, babe. I want you to come without worrying about anything except your orgasm. Come harder for me."

She started bucking again. I slammed into her, alternating between squeezing and spanking her lovely ass, heightening our passion with little surprises she couldn't ignore.

When the wood and springs knocking around beneath us were louder than her muffled screams, I knew I'd done my job.

"Come, baby. Grind your clit on this cock 'til you can't see anything but red."

My fingers meshed harder into her ass cheeks. I pulled her in, fucking the whole time, rubbing my pubic shield against her sweet cunt creaming all over my cock.

Her contractions started slow, and then exploded in raging waves.

I grinned, happy she'd finally let go. I pushed her deeper into the pleasure, throwing my hips up into hers, fucking like a demon. June screamed so loud I'm sure it echoed through the clubhouse, and I didn't give a fuck.

I wouldn't have stopped power fucking her if all my brothers heard every whimper, every breathless howl. *Especially* if they heard it, listening to the shrill sounds of a woman they'd never have because she was mine now.

"Holy fucking shit. Here we go!"

Growling, I spiked up into her. My balls tightened and ripped lose, sending their contents blasting out of my cock.

I held onto her ass so hard it hurt. I came deep, raking her pussy like I owned it, fucking through our spasms until our muscles were completely fucking drained.

June's soft hair grazing my chest woke me from my stupor. I looked down and saw her collapsed against me, spent and breathing in badly needed air.

"You see that, babe?"

"Hm?"

"I know how to wipe away the bad shit. I'll work your sweet mind just like I work your body," I said, giving her full ass one more squeeze. Damn, I loved that ass.

"It's all but official. You're mine, June. Property of Maverick."

She gasped and shivered a little in my arms. Finally, she looked up.

"How does that sound?" I ran a finger beneath her chin, going up around her ear.

"Pretty fucking good. Or maybe you've rattled my brain too much for my own good." Her smile was faint, but there was no mistaking it.

Was she blushing like a schoolgirl? Shit.

I smiled back, but her lips calling, lonely and hot. I moved in, claiming what belonged to me with another kiss.

Throttle arrived with a bigger presence than I expected on Friday, as promised.

I was looking pretty sharp in my freshly cleaned cut. The clubhouse had never looked better. Got the guys to lay off the whiskey and pussy long enough to pick up mops and bring in new furniture.

They whined about doing Prospects' work, but I wasn't complaining, and told them they'd better get fucking used to it. This charter was in no shape to start recruiting yet.

Guys from the Dakota crew arrived on bikes, SUVs, and even a big ass RV.

"What's with the warship?" I asked, as soon as Throttle parked his Harley and shook my hand.

"Brought along the family," he said. "Also looks more legit when we're hauling tons of shit you need in the trucks behind it. Telling any nosy badges it's a camping trip is a lot easier when it looks like one."

I nodded. The man didn't get to be President of the mother charter by being stupid or lucky, no matter what folks said when he was first voted in.

"It's not a lie for once either. We really are heading out to Oregon for a couple weeks after I see this house in order. Most of the guys along for the ride will stay here." He motioned to the dozen men behind him, most smoking or lounging around their bikes before they followed us inside.

"Everybody needs a vacation," I said.

"Yeah. But first, where's your meeting room? I want to get this shit settled and over with."

I stopped by the bar to pick up some glasses and a bottle of Jack, and then we were in my office.

"They'll expect you to wait and play defense. Warlock filled me in on what Blaze said. Told me about your deception. It won't throw them off for long. They're coming as soon as you refuse to turn over their cut of strip club profits."

"I know," I said. I picked up my glass and knocked down the whiskey in one shot. "I'm not gonna let it get that far. Soon as they know we double-crossed them, they're getting hit so hard they won't be able to stand up."

Throttle took his sips slow, steady, rolling the whiskey in his mouth. I always downed mine straight, ignoring the taste and looking for the burn. Wasn't sure how or why he did pulls like a fucking wine connoisseur.

"I appreciate a good offense. Learned the hard way that's the way to go when we beat the Skulls last year. Knocking these fuckers flat before they do the same to you is the only way to go. You need to take out their Missoula branch before the whole fucking tree falls from the West, right on your heads."

He clapped his hands. I stared.

Throttle had a knack for dramatic leadership at times. I didn't fault him here. This was a game with no room for error. Any slip ups had a grim finality as sharp and fast as his hands came together.

Throttle raised his glass to his lips again. "One more thing. Don't hesitate to attack and let yourself get distracted. I made that mistake in Cassandra, and it almost got a lot of people killed, including my old lady."

"Good advice. Doubt any of this is going down neat and smooth."

"It won't," he said sharply. "But when it's all over and you're leaving their carcasses to the crows, you won't regret a thing. I've made my mistakes. But I don't waste a second anymore looking back. Neither should you."

"Say the word and I'll give my guys the go ahead to start unloading and inventorying everything you've dropped here."

He stood up, shook my hand, and we were out.

Later, at the bar, I noticed his strange absence from the rest of the boys chattering and screwing around. I went out for some fresh air and saw the lights on in the RV.

Throttle and his girl were behind a thick shade. Next to them, his newborn son bounced in a little baby chair.

I balled fists at my sides and breathed deep. The man who headed our mother charter was between two worlds now. One foot in his MC, and the other in a happy family life.

Until lately, I never thought those worlds could co-exist. Not comfortably, anyway.

Now it was beckoning to me, and family world was one seductive bitch I couldn't turn down.

I'd never admit it in the open, but I wanted exactly what he had. Hell, I needed it.

Maybe I'd had my fill of being the outsider after too many years heading the Nomads, riding all over hell without a place to call home. Or maybe I'd just met the right girl.

Hold tight, babe, I thought. *The sooner we're all safe from the bears breathing down our necks, the better.*

I'm gonna wipe away everything those bastards did and give you a life worth living.

VII: Promises Made in Flesh (June)

The clubhouse shook with manly laughter, girlish giggles, and way too much whiskey for the next three days. I could barely get any shut eye when I came back late from Python's booming strip club.

It was like one long party that didn't wind down until the wee hours. The atmosphere wasn't somber like I expected for men going off to war. More like one wild celebration, one big explosion of feasting and hedonism, just in case some guys never made it back.

I was outside enjoying the rare quiet on the morning the Cassandra President was due to embark.

The door to the garages opened. Several guys from this charter plus North Dakota stepped out, Maverick among them.

Smiling quietly, I watched as he talked to men and directed them to the big storage room they'd set up in the garages. Part of me didn't want to know what the hell they were keeping there.

But I liked watching him, especially so early when everybody was filled with energy. Maverick was at his best – and his achingly sexiest – when he looked like the commander he was.

"You really like him, don't you?"

I turned toward the voice and saw a small girl cradling a baby in her arms. Throttle's girl, Rach.

Just looking at her, it was hard to believe she'd delivered the healthy boy, let alone that she was old lady to the most powerful man in the whole MC.

Guess that made her First Old Lady, come to think of it.

"Who?" I stood, smiling at her infant son. Seeing the baby turned everything all warm and fuzzy in my blood.

It was weird to have a baby here, but a good kind of weird. He was such a contrast to the brutal ice normally surrounding my life.

"Maverick. You don't have to play shy with me, girl. I've seen the way you look at him. Same way I still look at Jack."

"He's pretty nice," I agreed. What else could I say? "Surprised me when I found out he's got a softer side than the tough, mean biker Prez everybody else sees…"

"Don't they all?" Rach smiled, pulling her son tighter. "It only gets better when you see these cavemen around babies. Maybe you'll find out one day."

"Maybe. Maverick kinda…asked me to be his old lady." I tensed up, unsure why the hell I was telling her all this.

"That's wonderful!" Rach whispered. "You're going to fit in great. I can tell you're not exactly new to this lifestyle."

I managed a small, dark smile. "I've got my doubts."

"Don't. You've found the right man. No matter how crazy or scary things get, remember that. Put your faith in him to protect you and make you happy, and he will. Jack and I have our spats, but at the end of the day he loves me like nobody else ever will, and that's all that matters."

I started to regret starting up this conversation. I looked Rach up and down. Old lady to a powerful President or not, she looked even younger than me.

Did I really want to be taking advice from a skinny little girl who'd probably just gotten into bed with the big cheese and made him fall for those big bright eyes?

"The MC's like family once you really get into it," Rach continued. "If yours is anything like mine, then you grow attached to all the guys and their girls. I was happy just to see Tank again. Real glad he's doing well out here and – "

I raised my hands. "Respectfully, Rach, you're talking about a lot of things I already know. Maybe some things I'm not sure I ever want to know as well as you do."

The happy glow on her face wilted. She shrugged.

"Fine. I just like to see folks who are meant to get together do it sooner so they don't have to suffer through the shit Jack and I did. I'm trying to do you a favor before you mess up like me."

"I don't think we're anything alike," I said, ready to turn and walk away.

Rach's stare turned colder, holding me in place. "No?"

I shook my head. She stepped closer to me, slow and weirdly out of character. If she wasn't holding an infant, I would've sworn she was trying to intimidate me.

"You're wrong. Throttle almost helped me put a bullet through my asshole father's head for selling me into slavery. He killed for me, and I've never tried to wash away the blood on my hands. I embrace it." She leaned in close, her voice a low, sinister whisper. "You're not the only girl who's been through some shit and then fell for an MC President. If I can wise up and trust my heart, so can you."

I flinched. I stared at her, numb with surprise, unmoving. She broke away, heading for the RV, humming some soft, sad tune to her baby.

Deep down, the strange girl was right.

I feared turning over complete control to Maverick and becoming his old lady. But when I reached deep and thought hard, I feared life without him even more.

You can't let the past hold you back. Listen to her.

Later in the evening, the Dakota crew was heading out, minus a couple guys they'd left behind. I stood next to Maverick for the grand sendoff. Funny how I already looked like his old lady in public.

Throttle was on his bike at the head of the small column, and he waved to us when he switched on the ignition.

"You remember what we walked about. Next time I come through here, I wanna camp out in Missoula. The only Grizzlies we need to worry about better be the big brown ones up in the mountains." Several guys laughed. "You'll take care of business, Maverick. This MC's in good hands."

I looked over my shoulder. Maverick's brother Blaze didn't look so sure about the last part. I didn't totally get all the tension between them, but it seemed like it was getting better lately.

They faced a common threat. No time for dick waving, right?

Several big, masculine fingers brushed mine. I looked down and saw Maverick enveloping my hand in his.

He was smiling, and I returned his grin. Out here in the crisp morning air, standing with the man I loved and a bunch of biker brothers in high spirits, it didn't feel like ill winds were blowing in.

The RV followed the bikes and SUVs, the last big vehicle to leave the clubhouse's lot.

Inside, the shade was pulled up on the main window. I saw Rach, grinning and waving to all the men like a princess making her grand departure.

She wasn't looking up and down the crowd, though. Her eyes were fixed on me. I lifted my free hand and returned the gesture, if only to be polite.

Just before it turned out of view, Rach tapped her chest. I wasn't sure what the hell she was getting at. Then I realized it was her heart, a sharp jab right there, as if it say, *Remember.*

Maverick's hand tightened on mine. In his sweet, strong grip, I was completely safe, no matter what kind of hell was coming in torrents.

I breathed deep, filling my lungs before I climbed in the beaten up Ford they'd loaned me for work.

Today wouldn't be so bad. And just now, I had a weird feeling being his old lay wouldn't be either.

"Miss Daniels? I...I don't think I can go on tonight."

I spun in my chair, away from the little laptop that contained the club's info. I knew that kind of hollow tremor, and it caused me to sigh even before I saw her.

Great, here it comes. Another girl bowing out because she let guys buy her too many free drinks. Probably sprained an ankle tumbling into their laps...

Why can't I find girls who just do their jobs and go home without any drama?

My heart leaped into my throat when I took a good look at Saffron in the dim light. Something red and slightly purple circled her eye.

Jumping out of my chair, I closed the space between us. "Holy shit! Who did this to you?"

"A new guy I never seen before," she whimpered. "Not anybody with the Devils patch."

I closed my mouth. She'd already answered my second question, however unlikely it seemed.

The Devils weren't brutes to their women, no matter how rough the guys at the clubhouse got with their new play sluts. There was only one MC I knew about who treated girls like shit…

"Jesus. Follow me to the vending machine so we can get something cold on it."

She trailed behind me like a kid, sniffing away tears. We didn't have an ice machine anywhere near my poor excuse for an office.

I threw in some dollars and bought a couple cans of root beer. Saffron took them in her little hands and held them to her eye socket, wincing at the cold.

"Jesus!" I gasped again. This night was turning into something else. "I'm gonna ask you again. What happened?"

"It was a big, gruff guy in leather. Thought he was with the Devils at first, but the patches were all wrong. Should've called security right then, but I didn't notice he was an outsider until after he hit me in the face."

Fucking Grizzlies. Here!

I pressed my nails into my palms. It took a little pain to defuse the anger boiling in my blood.

"Why did he hit you?"

"Said he wanted to talk to you, Miss Daniels. Something about owing them some money he'd come to collect. He sounded half-drunk and I didn't like the way he spoke. Guy had a gross bandage around his head.

Fucking thing looked like it hadn't been washed in days…" She shifted the cold can on her face. "Anyway, I wasn't gonna send him back here. Didn't take too kindly to it when I told him he'd have to set up a meeting."

"Pssh, nobody sets up meetings with me." I took her limp hand in mine and squeezed. "But you did the right thing. Where's this asshole now?"

"He hit me when I was off the stage, getting some water at the bar. I had some fans around…they grabbed him and held him until George came."

George was the big senior bouncer we'd hired. I doubted he had half the combat skills of anybody in the MC, but he was a large man who knew how to throw his weight around.

"Don't know what happened after that…my head was spinning and I was seeing stars. Came right back to you to ask if I could get the night – "

"You're off," I finished for her. "Sit down and rest. Go home and take care of that eye. I can get somebody to drive if you're not up for it."

She sucked at her bottom lip, nibbling nervously on it. "Actually…can I spend the night at the clubhouse? Or at least get a couple guys from the club at my apartment? I'm afraid to be alone after what happened here…"

"I'll ask." She had my sympathy. Truly.

"No need to. She's welcome to stay at my clubhouse tonight and however many nights she needs." Maverick stepped up next to us.

My jaw almost hit the floor. How long had he been there, listening to us?

"Did you hear what she said? Grizzlies here, coming to collect money…"

His eyes went dark and serious. "I know all about it. Come on. Have somebody look after her and I'll send Blaze or Shatter around in a little while to pick her up."

"Wait, wait, where are we going?"

Maverick wrapped his hand around my wrist and pulled me along. I kept asking as he yanked me out the back door, into the darkness.

A truck was waiting for us out back. He walked straight toward the passenger door.

"What? No bikes?" Now I really didn't know what the hell was going on, but it was scaring me.

"Not for this," he said coldly. "You can ride between Tank and I. We've got a short run to make into the boonies."

I looked behind me. Pink Unlimited's bright burgundy and neon lights were warm, inviting, and safe compared to the mysterious darkness up ahead.

Trust him. Trust your heart.

I remembered Rach's words. Muscling up my strength and my faith, I squeezed his hand and climbed into the truck ahead of him.

Tank nodded politely from the driver's seat, and then Maverick was in behind me. The door slammed shut.

"Let's go," he ordered. "She's been waiting a long time for this, and so have I."

He wasn't fucking kidding about riding into the boonies. I'd been a Montana girl all my life, and even went camping a few times before Mom completely lost herself to drugs and Dad gave himself to the wrong brotherhood.

We bounced up and down in our seats as Tank guided us along little mountain roads. These were narrow paths without much paving, and even fewer guard rails. If a logging truck came trundling down the road and a bad driver lost control, it was a drop for hundreds of feet, straight into the wilderness.

"Jesus! Fuck," I whispered, clawing at my man's big, tattooed arm.

Next to us, Tank chuckled. "It's okay. Drove on much worse than this outside Kandahar."

We rumbled on, into the darkness, the eerie silence inside the truck broken only by the big tires struggling along the narrow paths.

When I mustered up the courage to look outside the window again, we were descending, into what looked like a clearing for a park. Or hell, maybe just some God forsaken place where nature had forgotten to sprout cedars and rocks.

Tank rolled into a natural shoulder formed by jagged rocks off to the side. Without a word, he shut the truck off and Maverick tugged gently on my hand, leading me to follow him outside.

There was another vehicle there with its lights off. Empty.

We all got out. Closing our doors echoed for miles.

Tank's huge shadow was slightly ahead of us. I saw him stop at the place where the road veered toward a stream down a little path. Several other guys were there – three maybe – one of them crouched down on the ground.

My heart raced. I looked up pleadingly at Maverick. He refused to meet my eyes in the darkness, and just kept going.

When we met up with the other group, I saw it was Hypno and another guy I barely recognized, one of the men who'd stayed behind from the Dakota crew.

"Pick the asshole up and carry him further back. Straight toward the stream. Good place to flush this fucking turd after we're done with him."

I forced myself to look down at the shape huddled on the ground. I recognized Scoop instantly.

His nasty body twitched nervously. Muffled noises came out of his mouth around the gag stuffed into it.

He looked like he'd been roughed up, and the bandage Saffron mentioned was jerked lower, covering his eyes like a thick blindfold. His forehead was scratched raw, almost dented at the place where I'd smashed him with the bottle.

The night seemed to swell and swallow up everything else, including me.

I should've gotten in touch with God, or just my more reasonable human instincts. It shouldn't have been so easy to embrace the merciless pulse throbbing in my blood.

But this man and his disgusting VP had butchered any chance of forgiveness years ago.

I could only look at Maverick with an awe-struck smile in the darkness. He turned his head, wearing a stern expression on his face, but there was no smile.

Scoop screamed into his gag as the Prairie Devils picked him up. They carried him by the arms, dragging his legs over rocks and tangled branches. We moved behind him, stepping carefully into the perfect blackness, into hell.

Jesus. He's like a giant cat bringing me a prize after hunting.

Only I'm not sick and grossed out. I'm happy.

What the fuck is wrong with me?

Clara's terrified face flashed in my mind, over and over. I remembered her blood curdling screams when the ruthless creep in front of me ripped off her clothes.

Adrenaline and bad memories collided, punching me straight in the brain. I puffed angrily, gathering breath, forcing away the tears.

Maverick's warm hand on mine constricted. "Drop him right there, by the water."

The men complied. Scoop crumpled on the shore, alternately screaming and sobbing into his gag. Nothing answered him except the cold, steady burble of the rocky stream.

Maverick broke away from holding my hand. He walked to him, grabbed his greasy hair, and jerked him up by the head.

It was a clear night, and the half-moon yielded enough light to see the terror inscribed on his face.

"Remember her, asshole?" Maverick growled, low and demanding into his ear. "She's one reason we had to bring your sorry ass out here tonight. Reason number two is thinking you'd get away with fucking over my club."

Maverick's eyes flashed wickedly. I jumped as he brought a gun out of his jacket and smashed Scoop's head from behind, tearing away the blindfold and popping out the gag in the process.

"Oh, God. Please, please, man. Don't be stupid. We can work something out. Anything!"

Rage prickled at my skin. This demon had scared me plenty of times, but now I wasn't afraid. I walked up to him, ready to confront the beast who'd left me alone and broken for so many years.

I wasn't alone anymore.

"God? Where was he when you fucking raped my sister?" I screamed, and then stopped.

My voice echoed through the trees. I wasn't expecting it to be so loud.

"Don't worry, babe. Nothing but little hunting cabins here for miles. We checked. They aren't occupied this time of year. Nobody will hear this fuck scream or cry like a little bitch. His life was over the minute we pulled up." Maverick's words were all I needed to hear.

Scoop stopped yelling and got quiet. Deadly calm crossed his face, as if he finally realized how hopeless his situation really was.

I looked into familiar eyes, suddenly brimming with sadistic darkness. This was the face I was used to, the rapist and the killer.

"You want to put this sack of shit out of his misery or should I?" Maverick looked at me behind him, offering me his gun.

I didn't say anything. I was too lost staring into Scoop's predatory eyes, interfacing with one of the only other minds on the planet who shared Clara's last bitter moments.

For me, it was death, the moment I lost my twin sister and a part of myself forever. For this monster, it was a joy, one more bitch he savaged with glee.

"Heh. You look just like her, you know." He let out a dull laugh. "Least I'm gonna go to hell remembering your sweet little sissy crying and hollering as I shoved my cock up her – "

Scoop's head exploded. Maverick's lips were peeled back, baring his teeth like a feral animal. A few reddish flecks sprayed his face, and he wiped his forehead with one hand.

Maverick lowered the gun away from the man's shattered temple and stood.

My tormenter began to fall as soon as he let go. Not fast enough.

I ran forward, howling like a wildcat as I kicked his dead body square in the chest.

Then I stood over him, staring at his vacant eyes. Thick red gore gushed from the hole in his head, coating the rocks beneath our feet.

A gentle hand fell on my shoulder and squeezed. Maverick had every right expecting me to breakdown. I didn't blame him, but he was wrong.

I turned coldly and pressed myself into his arms. "You delivered. Thank you."

"Babe, for you, I'd execute every last twisted fuck wearing their patch. Did this one with you because I knew it's personal. You deserved this."

My heart swelled. I'd just watched as he murdered a monster in front of me, and I felt something I never expected.

Real love. My heart throbbed, so airy it almost made me dizzy, blood flowing through my veins like warm honey.

I loved him before, but this was something else. An intensity I'd never known for another human being throbbed inside me as I leaned in, inhaling his scent, feeling his warm skin.

His muscular body stiffened against me. While he held me like this, alive and in love, it was easy to forget the despicable corpse at our feet.

Until he gave the orders.

"Boys, get over here and clean this shit up. Tank, you're with me again. Let's beat it to the clubhouse. Fucking creepy out here in the boonies at night."

So help me, I laughed.

"Just one more thing…" he said.

I waited for him as he knelt next to Scoop's body. He pulled out a big knife and stretched the dead man's jacket, then punched the blade through it and began cutting.

When he was through, he held up the big Grizzlies patch, complete with its bottom rocker.

"Catch, June," he said, throwing the material into my hands. "Normally, the MC keeps a trophy like this for ourselves. But as President, I'm gonna make one little exception."

Hypno and the Dakota man came up to the body and looked at their leader. Maverick gave them a severe look and guided the torn patch to my jean pocket.

"Don't look so glum, boys. By the time we're done with these fucks, there'll be plenty more where that came from."

Maverick and I walked slowly to the truck with Tank trailing in behind us. I rested my head on his shoulder during the drive along the tiny paths. It wasn't so frightening the second time around, or I was just riding too high on cloud nine to care.

He'd proven me wrong tonight.

I thought losing Clara had shattered me into a thousand pieces, many of which would never, ever return. True, I'd never be whole after my terrible time with the Grizzlies.

But with him, I wasn't empty anymore. I had a man who loved me, who'd fucking kill to protect me, and it filled me with a rosy hope that wasn't displaced forever like I'd thought.

My head was still buzzing and half-foggy when we got to the clubhouse. Had the last two hours really happened?

The smell of whiskey and seasoned meat hit me in the face as I stepped in. Maverick held the door for me like a lady making a grand entrance, a silly follow-up to the major chivalry he'd done earlier.

I smiled and stepped inside. For once, the club felt like home, even with three times as many guys hanging around to support the new war effort.

"Blaze!" Maverick called, searching for his brother at the bar.

I followed him in, and we found the VP in the corner, sitting with a very familiar face.

My eyes bugged out when I saw him with Saffron, way too close for comfort. I wasn't oblivious to what a crazy womanizer he was, and I ran forward to make sure he hadn't put any moves on her.

My stripper wasn't a saint, but no girl wanted to be hit on after she'd been smashed in the face by a stinking scum bag.

Blaze looked up at us, surprised and embarrassed. Saffron's expression mirrored his.

I saw his hand pull back a small bag of ice he'd been holding gently on her face.

Holy shit. He hadn't been priming her up for something nasty after all – he was seriously helping her.

"Yeah, what's up, Prez?" He looked at us, half-annoyed as he turned the ice pack over to Saffron.

"Got an announcement to make. I need you and everybody else who's still up right now for witnessing. We can do it right later on," Maverick looked at me. "But this can't wait."

Blaze's irritation melted away. He looked curious and confused.

"What is this, Aaron?"

Maverick grabbed my hand and wedged it to his hard chest. "I'm making June my old lady today. Claiming her. I'm tired of my guys thinking I've got two competing interests. Today, those interests become one."

With a flick of his hand, he pulled me fully against him, wrapping his free arm tight around my waist. I flushed. Nobody had ever made such a public spectacle over me before.

"Besides…I love this girl, brother. I'm not scared to say it. I don't give a fuck if you and the rest of the club want to giggle and jabber behind my back. This is fucking real, and the two of us know it."

He kissed me. Hard and fast, a full on kiss meant for claiming. It cut through me, deep in his embrace, filling me with raw heat.

Took a lot to tear himself away. I sensed the reluctance in the way he moved. Everything about the way he moved said he wanted to be one with me – same thing I ached for at the deepest level.

"You ready for this, babe?"

We'd shared flesh and spilled blood together. Nothing erased that, and I couldn't imagine living without him anymore.

Yes. I'm ready.

I threw my arms around his neck and smiled. "Never thought I would be. You proved me wrong. Wouldn't be the first time."

Blaze's gaze was still on us. Saffron sat next to him, her good eye wide, her astonished lips cracked open. Several guys further down the bar were watching us too.

Slowly, Maverick's brother stood, and looked right at us. The stony expression betrayed nothing.

Then he clapped us both on the shoulders at once.

"Congratulations, brother!" he said to Maverick, before turning to me. "I had my doubts about you, June. I thought you were distracting my brother, threatening this MC. I was wrong. You shared our troubles before he called you his old lady. Once you've shared yourself with us and carried our burdens, you're a part of this MC forever. There's no one better I'd like to see him with."

"Thanks," I muttered, too surprised to say it with confidence.

Blaze stepped away, cupped his hands over his mouth, and yelled. "We need everybody's attention! So put down the Jack and stop jacking off beneath the tables. Put your fucking eyes on your gracious host and our President, Maverick of the Nomads."

"Python too!" Maverick corrected.

Several loud laughs rang out. We had a serious audience now, the dozen or so guys there focused entirely on us. Maverick pushed me tighter to his muscles, his heart.

"Prairie Devils are a brotherhood," he began. "Some of you here tonight don't know me that well one-on-one, but you're witnesses and brothers one and the same. Devils take what they want. Devils give their word. I'm not gonna bore you with a long bullshit speech because I've already waited too long for this.

"Tonight, I'm taking June Daniels as my old lady. My property. She's off limits to anyone except me. If anyone has a problem with that, then they'll have to go through my fucking fists to file their complaint. Treat her with the respect an old lady deserves, and spread the word to every brother in every charter. This woman is *mine*."

His voice deepened to a growl. The bass notes ran right through my flesh and hit me deep.

Shit. I shifted my thighs. My panties were twice as soaked listening to the strict possession in his voice, the way he called me his property.

The hand around my waist turned a little more possessive. Men roared their approval, including Blaze right next to us. His enthusiasm kept surprising me, its loudness filling my ear.

My lips were pursed, full, and ready for another kiss before his mouth covered mine. His tongue darted out, taking what he was entitled to, stroking mine the way he'd soon be fucking me.

Breaking the kiss left me breathless and trembling in his arms. God, I was totally going to pieces here, right in front of all these rugged bikers.

"Blaze, hold down the fort. Business can wait until morning."

"Sure can." His brother grinned and gave him a quick salute. "I'm man enough to admit my mistakes, brother. I'm glad we're on the same page again."

"So am I."

"Hey, aren't I supposed to get inked up or something now?" I asked.

He shot me a look that left no doubt about what our next move would be. "Yeah, but we'll save that for later. Right now, all I care about is reminding you how deep you're in with me. Forever."

Maverick picked me up and held me in his arms effortlessly. We headed straight for his room. I flattened my hands on his broad, beautiful chest when we turned the corner, ready and eager to feel him all over me.

He kicked the door open and then shut it with another twist of his leg.

We toppled to the bed together and got naked in seconds. Maverick had his big, strong face buried between my legs before I so much as braced for it.

He licked. He sucked. He tongued me deep the same way he kissed – absolutely possessive.

His touch had grown a whole lot stricter since he officially owned me. But I loved every squeeze of his fingers and flick of his tongue. Hadn't believed he could ratchet up the passion higher than before.

Like everything about him, I was wrong.

And he proved it in every stroke arcing lightning up my core. My hips rocked against his mouth, thighs pinched tight, one notch away from completely giving myself over.

I held back a little because the climax building wasn't anything I'd felt before. What he unleashed in this bed before was awesome, but this was a fucking tornado.

It moved with its own energy and fury. Unstoppable as it was delectable. When he found my clit, drawing it deep in his mouth for an assault with his tongue, I couldn't stop it.

"Maverick! Aaron!" I screamed, smashing my hips to his rough mouth.

Orgasm came, blinding, sticky, unbearably hot. He held my legs down, keeping me spread as he continued to work lightning into me.

Somewhere in the ecstasy, I recognized the way I'd screamed both his names. His dual identities pinpointed what made him so insanely attractive, and dangerous as hell too.

I had a lion between my legs, a man who loved as well as he killed.

I didn't have a choice anymore. My body decided for me, and so had my heart, throwing my worthless senses to the curb. The pleasure he delivered in wave after knee trembling wave told me he was welcome there anytime he wanted.

My love. My life. My guardian.

When I glided off the cloud, he lay next to me, surrounding me in his immense arms. He licked my cream from his lips before kissing me again, and I tasted the phantom of my own sultry fire on his lips.

"Hope all that coming didn't put you to sleep, babe. We're just getting warmed up." Dark demands glowed in his eyes – dirty, delightful things I couldn't say no to. "Spread your legs. I'm not done getting your pussy ready for me."

I whimpered when his hand went between my legs. He cupped my slick mound, and then pushed two strong fingers inside, thrusting deep, gentler than the way he'd taken me before.

"You're giving this all up to me now aren't you, old lady?"

"Yes!" I hissed, squirming as his thumb brushed along my clit. "It's yours. Anything."

Holy shit. Who are you, June?

The whiny little voice in the back of my head was squashed a second later when I looked deep into his bright eyes. They told me exactly who I was, who I'd become.

I was Maverick's old lady, his property, a willing slave to the man who'd delivered me. He'd brought me back from the dead, and now I wanted to give him everything worthy of a miracle.

Giving up every last inch of my flesh seemed a small price to pay. Maybe too small to ever thank him for what he'd done, what he was still going to do.

"Fuck, babe. So tight…so wet…all for me. Good girl."

He drew his fingers out and gave my swollen lips a quick smack. I jumped, jolted with surprise and pleasure.

"The tattoo that tells the world you're mine can go anywhere you want. Shoulder, arm, neck, I don't give a shit. Long as you see it, and it reminds you this is mine now." He wiggled his fingers, opening me like a flower, before slipping them inside. "Morning. Noon. Night. Fucking Twilight. You keep this sweet pussy warm and wet and ready, because I haven't even begun to fuck it."

His words were turning me into a puddle. I rocked my hips, fucking his hand, amazed I could be ready for more so quickly.

I hadn't wanted to admit it, but before all this, I'd been pretty fucking starved for sex. Now my young body wanted to make up for the years I'd lost with the Grizzlies.

Maverick's cock pressed angrily on my hip. I threw my head back, kissed him, and reached down.

Oh no, you don't. You don't get to make me come again without feeling what you've got down there…

Fuck. Wow. So hard. So ready.

I squeezed his shaft. He pumped his hips, moving deeper into my fist, grunting a little when my fingers pinched around his length.

Hot pre-come dripped onto my skin. I hissed raw pleasure, even as his strokes between my legs became more erratic. It was easy to forget how big and perfect he really was.

I clenched him tight to remind myself, circling the thick ridge of his cock's head with his own slickness. He grunted again, and then pulled away, moving on top of me.

His fingers were quickly replaced by his cock as he shoved it against my opening. His eager head rubbed my clit before he moved down.

Looking me straight in the eyes, he forced his way in, taking the throne of flesh he owned in my body. Sparks exploded in my brain, blinding and numerous as stars.

"Wrap your long, beautiful legs around me, babe. I riding fucking hard tonight. I treat what's mine very well, but I also like to play with it *rough*. Stretched to its limits."

"Mmmm. You can be as big and bad as you want," I purred. "Long as you don't break me."

He leaned down, thrusting deep and holding his cock against my womb. I squirmed, impaled on his length, wondering if this was some new delicious torture he'd cooked up.

"Babe, be careful what you wish for...you just might get it. If you break, I'll put you back together again. I promise."

His hips lurched forward. He held my head as I thrashed back and forth, losing myself in his savage thrusts, feeling his massive length pummel and stretch like he promised.

Over and over and over, he threw himself into me, deeper and harder.

Our hips collided. My clit hummed, a small pink lightning rod overflowing with energy, sending its rabid, primal pulse straight through every muscle.

He grunted like an animal as he fucked me, rougher than ever before. Desperate jerks throttled through his hips, driving into me.

The old bed matched my screams, sharing the hammer blows he leveled between my legs. We had to find our release together, brutal and inevitable.

Who was I fucking kidding? I couldn't last long like this. He was in complete control of when I came, and how furious it would be.

I barely had my arms and legs pinched tight around his huge, tattooed body before I erupted.

"Aaron…Aaron…fuck!" I bit my lip.

My nerves lit up like a Christmas tree. Lungs, heart, and brain all shut down, blasted to silence by electrified blood.

Everything below my waist spasmed in one jerk. My heels jabbed hard at his muscle, as hard as they could, but still they didn't make a dent.

"Yeah, babe. Let go and surf. Ride this fucking wave." His steady growl made me tense harder. "Oh, fuck!"

His breath hitched with mine. I spasmed again, slow and foaming like a whirlpool. Pure fire bathed my brain, my blood, rending my entire being into ash.

I erupted into him. My inner fire lapped at my clit and nipples like nothing else, puckering muscles deep inside me.

I rocked. I came. I loved him.

Black and red and white spiraled in my vision. Everything faded except the steady slap and thrust of his cock deep inside me.

Uninhibited.

I was barely coming to earth when he shifted. He pulled my legs up high over his waist, changing the angle between us, all the better to sink to my quaking depths.

No rest for the wicked. Certainly not lovers drunk on lust.

When he started fucking me again, whole galaxies filled my eyes. He punched down hard, hooking his hips perfectly to mine. Our flesh slapped louder than the bed spring's banshee screams, but only half as loud as the feral noises pouring out my mouth.

A wet, steady, and very fucking hot tempo filled the entire world. Or if not the world, then at least our bodies, echoing in heartbeats synchronized for mad release.

I reached up and ran my fingernails down his chest, raking his tattooed flesh. What would the huge Devils icon on his rock hard breasts look like with my grooves cut there?

I scratched again, both hands, moving my nails down his beautiful body like a cougar sharpening her claws. Maverick reared up, never slowing his thrusts even once.

He reached behind my head and fisted my hair, pulling it hard.

He lowered his face and whispered. "Play time's over, babe. Scratches fade. I'll fucking fill you up until you're leaking me for days, tasting these lips even when you don't want to."

Dirty words. They pushed me right over the edge and I started to pant, one more thrust or brush of the clit away from coming yet again.

Then he stopped, as if he knew, giving me one more round of torture. His lips found mine and kissed deep.

No, more than deep. He totally smothered me with his tongue, forcing it aggressively past my lips, holding down mine.

His hands pinned down my arms. He started to move again, slow and wicked, playing on the suffocating bliss building in my body.

I almost bit him when I came. But he knew how to hold me open, how to tame my body to work with him. He was the one who sucked at my bottom lip, holding it like an animal with his teeth, mating my flesh with his.

His thrusts picked up as my cunt spasmed around his length. They came fast, violent, and then shuddered to a screaming stop.

Those big hands pinched my wrists hard. He growled straight into my mouth, a kiss of roaring fire, and he exploded deep inside me.

My body jerked, finding a sharper release in his come.

I fully opened for him, inside and out. I stroked his lips with mine, and my greedy sex convulsed around him, milking his rippling cock.

Full body shudders aligned, and so did the stars. I couldn't see, smell, or feel anything but him.

I finally understood what it was truly like to be fused to another, chained to a man in flesh and fire.

And I never, ever wanted to let go.

I blinked, and it was all over. He was at my side, holding me in his arms, the hot mess between our legs still steaming on our flesh.

"Love you, babe. Love you even more now that it's official."

I answered him with my kiss. "You have no idea. I love you."

We fucked several more times as night blurred into morning.

The next day, I slept like the dead, and barely woke up in time to shower and high tail it to the strip club.

The whole night at work, I buzzed, remembering the way we'd struck vengeance by putting down one of my sister's killers. Oh, and the sharp ache between my legs was pretty sweet too.

VIII: Consequences, Consequences (Maverick)

June was on my mind every hour as the mountain spring bloomed into early summer.

Days passed in a fine delirium, always in bed with my new old lady when my boys and I weren't out patrolling. Weirdly, the Grizzlies hadn't gotten the message I'd sent with their missing man yet, and that fucking worried me.

Still, all those worries vanished when I had her in my arms, staring deep into her eyes. Even better when she was underneath me. Mounting her like a buck in rut was even more fun with the new tattoo on her upper shoulder.

PROPERTY OF MAVERICK, PRAIRIE DEVILS MC.

Fuck me. I'd never get tired of seeing those words.

It was also a good opportunity to give our new tattoo parlor a trial run. The guy we'd hired did his job well. Had a good feeling I'd be adding more ink to my guns later in the year.

I smiled just thinking about them as I led my guys on the run up to Missoula, searching for enemy activity. There was nothing up there.

Sent Tank into town for a quick ride past their shitty clubhouse. He reported the fucking place looked run down and deserted. Nothing there but a couple of their bikes parked past the gate.

I gripped my bike hard and gritted my teeth. Didn't fucking like it. Not one bit.

Fuck you, Vulture. Fuck you for bringing my ass up here instead of leaving it where it belongs, in bed, between my old lady's legs. Fuck you for making me look over my shoulder, wondering when you're gonna hit back for burying that prick in the cold Montana soil.

Halfway to Python, we pulled over at a mountain overlook and waited for Tank to catch up. His bike skidded to a stop next to me and he yanked off his helmet.

"Nothing, boss. Again. Locals I talked to say those fuckers have been pretty light around there the past week. The liquor stores and smoke shops haven't seen anybody in leather except cowboys and a few old retired guys out for a ride."

I shook my head. "Those fucks definitely received the message. Just didn't think they'd react to it like this. We need to find them soon, before they link up with their buddies across state lines."

That's the way it should've worked. Of course, life is rarely so fucking easy and forgiving.

We'd just gotten into Python when I noticed the big black van behind Hypno and Shatter riding tail. I blinked my lights and switched on the radio.

"Blaze, this fucker's coming awful close. Go behind him. I want a clear read on the plates."

"I'm on it."

I watched my brother get in the other lane, preparing to hang back and let the van pass him. The van was quicker.

It rolled into the next lane and kissed my brother's ass, driving like a fucking maniac. Blaze had no choice except to floor it, before he wound up squashed like a bug on the bumper.

"Fuck! Everybody on the shoulder!"

Knew exactly what was coming, and there wasn't any time to get out of the way. My brother barely made it ahead of me before the van came roaring up beside us.

The door slid open. Gunfire sprayed out around us instantly in sharp rattling bursts. Bikes behind me weaved and rolled, and so did I, desperate to avoid the big rounds filling the air.

Nobody survives a hit from full auto rounds easily.

I glanced up, relieved Blaze was still in one piece, and so was I. The van sped on. Instinct wanted me to draw my gun and shoot after it. Wouldn't do any fucking good, though, and it was all too likely to get unwanted forces involved.

We'd been lucky to keep any badges out of our war. Needed to keep it that way too.

It was a miracle there was nobody else on the mountain road behind us. We all stopped, and I heard my guys yelling at each other several feet away.

One of the bikes was tipped over, and a man was down.

Fuck!

Blaze was right beside me as we moved our fucking feet as fast as we could. I got to the end of the line and saw Tank on the dirty ground, steady blood trickling out the huge gash in his side.

"Fucking shit! Somebody take off some clothes and seal up that fucking wound." I reached for my burner phone and flipped it open. "Wiley? Yeah, it's me. Bring the god damned truck around as fast as you can! We got a man down. Call that fucking contact we've got at the hospital too. I don't give a fuck if she's on her shift. Do it!"

The Dakota boys were left behind guarding the clubhouse. Now, I had to count on them to haul ass out here, and hopefully get him back to the clubhouse for fixing up before it was too late.

If it wasn't already.

Fuck. I forced myself to look at the man I'd only recently accepted as a brother.

It was strange and sickening to see the big guy passed out on the ground limp. Going a little whiter by the second.

We weren't far from Python at all. The truck came roaring up three minutes later, and the men carried a big sheet. They tied it around his waist and started to move him.

Wisdom says moving an injured man is a bad idea. Just then, I didn't give a single fuck.

We had to take the risk. The only way to save him, and ourselves, was to get him patched up at the clubhouse.

Carrying a man with serious gunshot wounds into the nearest hospital up in Missoula invited trouble. These patches always did. Cops would be on us like flies, maybe even the Grizzlies to finish mowing us down.

"Let's go!" I yelled, following the men to the truck. "Is the girl coming? Emma or whatever?"

"She's on her way, Prez. Told the guys to have the backroom all ready for her with the tools we stored for something like this."

I grabbed Tank's wrist and squeezed before he disappeared inside the truck. "Don't die on me, brother. We need every muscle ready to snap the Grizzlies fucking necks."

The other guys were on their bikes and ready to go when I got on mine. I rode ahead, leading them to the clubhouse.

As soon as my brother was okay, we had to regroup, and fast.

Letting the bears draw blood once was inexcusable. If it happened twice, there wouldn't be a third chance for any of us.

"You gotta go, babe. No arguments. It's club business!"

June came right to the clubhouse as soon as she heard about the shooting. I spent the evening drawing up plans to shut down the strip club and get her the fuck out of here. Nothing was safe until the Grizzlies were dealt with – especially the soft targets that meant the most to me and to my club.

I'd pulled her into the storage room. No updates on Tank's condition for the last hour, so it seemed as good a time to talk as any. He was in the little infirmary we'd set up in a spare room, tended by the nurse who was friendly with the club. She got plenty of good pay to be on call for us.

"What? You want to send me away unprotected?"

"You'll go with the bouncers, and maybe a couple Dakota boys. Head out to Bozeman until this shit's settled. If anything happened to you in the middle of this shit…"

I lost my words. Angry fists formed at my sides, rocks ready to smash in any face that dared threaten her.

"It's not all club business," she said, stepping toward me. "I was there by your side the night we killed Scoop. I watched you put a bullet in his rotten brain. You wouldn't have killed him if it weren't for me. That makes it my business too."

"Can't let you do that. Fuck, don't make me tie your hands and shove you in the fucking truck with my guys! I need you safe."

My cock twitched when I thought about her all tied up and vulnerable. Must've been the anxiety making me think such ridiculous shit, getting me hard at the worst possible time.

"Do it, and I'll find my way back here. Fact is you're shutting down my strip club and hunkering down. I'll be your old lady, Aaron, but I won't be fucking useless."

Damn her. Switching out my road name for my real name always forced me to pay attention when I should've given my men their orders and slammed the fucking door, leaving her there until it was time for evacuation.

"Pink Unlimited's *our* fucking business. Not yours. You just manage it. If I didn't pull the plug, the Grizzlies would've been happy to shoot it up or burn the damned place down. I saved us all from that, just like I'm trying to save your sweet ass now."

"Then let me stay here and help. I know you're way outnumbered."

I snorted. She had me there – wasn't sure how she overheard so much shit about our war. Too many of my guys must've been drunk and talking at the bar.

"You really think Tank'll be the last guy to get hurt in all this? What happens when Nurse Emma can't handle all the injuries, or when something happens and she's away?"

I shook my head. "You don't know shit about patching up wounds."

"I can learn. I'll do anything you say, but I'm not going away. I'm staying here and helping the club by keeping the guys you'd have on me for protection kept here too. I'm not afraid of blood, especially if it means taking out the Missoula Grizzlies once and for all."

"You're going," I insisted. "I'm the fucking President and your old man. That ink on your shoulder isn't just meant to be sweet and sexy. You're my god damned property, and don't forget it! I'll do what's best for you, June. It's my right."

The room shook with my voice. She blinked and took a step back, but she never broke, never took her eyes off mine.

"Try it. You'll have to drug me to keep me away. You can throw me in handcuffs and drive me a hundred miles, and I'll still do whatever it takes to come back. I won't be alone again, Maverick. Not where the Grizzlies are concerned. Putting Scoop in the ground was a good first step, but I'm not satisfied. Not by half. When you took me as an old lady, you promised to keep me at your side. I'm going to live and breathe that promise, even when you don't want to. You owe me vengeance, just like you promised, and I owe you my heart."

Fucking hell. She had me, and the dangerous glint in her eye said she'd really do everything she threatened.

Before Throttle left, he told me all about how his old lady was captured and nearly sold to some sick fuck when he tried to send her away to protect her.

I didn't want to admit it – really didn't fucking want to – but June had a point. Sending her away from this place didn't guarantee shit. If she decided to fight it the whole time, then I'd have a bigger fucking mess on my hands.

If she struck out on her own, and the Grizzlies got to her before this MC did…

My hands slammed down on the little table between us. She jumped.

"All right! You're staying here, and I mean right. Fucking. Here!" I jabbed my pointer finger on the old wood until it hurt. "You don't shake a leg outside this clubhouse unless I say so. And if you think about defying me on anything else, I'll bind you up without a second thought."

Except for imagining how damned sexy it'll be, I thought. I wanted to drown my stupid brain in Jack and make it shut the fuck up.

Damned shame I needed all my senses sharp and clear right now.

Slowly, June nodded. "Thank you," she whispered.

Our business here was done. Time to get back to the business of life and death between MCs. I grabbed her hand and led her out of the little room, shoving the door behind me so hard it banged like a gunshot.

"How is he?"

"He's stable, Mister President. Lost a lot of blood. He won't be in any shape to run around for the club soon...but I think he's going to be alright." Emma peeled away the cuff she used to measure Tank's blood pressure.

"Just call me Maverick. Listen, we got ourselves a situation. If he's not ready to move on his own, then I need you to move him. Tonight."

Emma looked stressed. She'd done a bang up job helping my brother cheat death. Only trouble was I needed her on standby for more shit bound to go down anytime.

"Move him? Where?"

Tank lifted his huge head and caught the nurse's eyes. "It's okay, boss. Feels like a bad flu. I can get up and move on my own..."

He tried to sit up higher, and grunted. I winced as he fell back, making the whole table squeal with his weight.

"Bullshit. Listen to the lady, Tank. You've already done plenty for this club. Right now, we need you to rest where you'll be safe."

"We both know he can't go to a hospital. You mean you want me to bring him...?" She stopped just short of saying it.

Home.

Emma shifted uncomfortably. Her cheeks looked bright and pinkish. Fuck, it was like watching a couple high school kids dance around an inevitable prom date.

"Do it," I ordered. "We'll pay you extra when all this is over. If he can be alone, I'm gonna need you back here ASAP. If things don't go our way, then Tank's probably not gonna be the last guy to get hurt."

The nurse nodded solemnly. Satisfied, Tank and I exchanged nods too, and I stepped outside the tiny infirmary. Way too fucking small for any of us, including a giant like him, but it would have to do.

Blaze came running up to me as soon as I was out. I threw my hands up because I swore he was gonna crash right into me.

"Whoa. Where's the fucking fire?"

"Up by Kalispell! Throttle's latest trial run up to Alberta got intercepted. Two Dakota boys and fifty pounds of coke in Grizzlies hands."

"Shit! He should've suspended the runs as soon as things ramped up. We don't control shit north of Missoula with the bears stalking us. Did they make it out?"

Blaze shook his head. "Bypassed the clubhouse this morning. The Grizzlies don't take prisoners if it won't do them any good. They were beaten and cut up, patches missing. Boys told me they were heading straight to Dickinson without stopping."

"I don't blame them. Has anyone gotten in touch with Cassandra?"

"Yeah." Blaze's brow wrinkled, telling me I wouldn't like what he was about to say. "Warlock, their VP, took it in stride. Told me he'd put a stop to more runs, but we better get this shit under control fast. Any way we need to."

"What about Throttle?"

"Nobody can reach him wherever the fuck they went way out in the wilds. Looks like you're alone on this one, Aaron." He made a fist and pounded me on the shoulder. "You're the President, and the head cheese is AWOL. It's not too late to change course if tackling the Grizzlies head on isn't looking so pretty."

"It's our only fucking choice. Don't see how we can do anything else at this point. Any news from Missoula?"

"Nothing since we hauled Tank back here. Keeping the scouting up there limited. Your orders. Locals say our buddies are still strangely absent."

I snorted with frustration. Didn't understand how the hell I was supposed to hit them if I couldn't even find them.

I'd been awake for three solid days since Tank was shot. My eyes were burning something fierce, and my head buzzed like I'd been knocked on my ass a few too many times.

Blaze followed me over to the bar and grabbed a drink. I poured myself a single shot of Jack, something to take the edge off all this shit.

There was no time to get drunk. On the other hand, a little medicine cleared the head, helped me think.

"Take over for awhile," I told him. "I'm gonna be fucking useless if I don't get some shut eye for a couple hours."

It was late. June didn't even hear me come in. She was curled up in bed, wearing the sexy new nightgown she'd gotten right before things went crazy.

I crashed, burying her in my arms. She murmured and shifted, spooning her sweet ass into my hips, instantly making me hard.

Couldn't wait until the bullshit outside this clubhouse was over. Holding her in the darkness, it seemed like a million miles away.

Outside, an uncertain hell and bloodshed waited. In here, snuggled up against my babe, it was heaven.

My phone rang sometime just before dawn. Must've taken two or three calls to get me out of my stupor.

I rolled and bolted up, stepping outside before I woke up June.

"It's Blaze," the voice said on the line. "We found the Grizzlies."

"Where?"

"Pink Unlimited."

It took a second for the meaning to click. "What? That fucking place is supposed to be shut down."

"It is, brother. You better come out here and see this for yourself."

I cursed. Listening to those angry words hiss back at me in the empty bar was the last thing I heard before I ran outside and grabbed my bike.

A short ride later, I pulled in next to the strip club. Those flashing lights up the road told me it wasn't gonna be pleasant. I pounded my Harley with my right fist, furious because I knew those fucks had gotten the drop on us again.

"What the fuck? How did this happen?" I practically spun my brother around by the neck when I found Blaze on the sidelines.

"The patrol crew caught them just in time. Shatter and the Dakota bros chased them off, but not before one of Vulture's fuckers threw a lighter. Whole fucking backside was soaked in gasoline and went up like a bomb."

"Motherfuckers!" I turned away from him, staring at the faint outlines of the mountains.

They took me away from this place, away from this insane guerrilla war with fucking barbarians. I took a good, long look at the mountains, knowing it was gonna be the last time to savor them before I was barraged with questions from the fire chief, insurance, and my own damned MC.

We didn't return to the clubhouse until early afternoon. June jumped out of our way when she saw us filing in, heading straight for the meeting room. Nobody was in any fucking mood for the drinks and snacks she sweetly offered.

"Not now, babe. Not this fucking century," I growled.

Knew I'd regret it later, but right now we had serious business on our plates. If something didn't change drastically very, *very* fast, then I'd be the first Prairie Devils' President in a generation to be chased out of my own territory.

I quietly vowed I wouldn't live that humiliation. Hell no.

It was the four full patch members in the room, along with ten Dakota boys, one of them offering to proxy for Tank if things came to a vote.

With everybody assembled, I stared at all the faces in silence, waiting to hear just how pissed my guys were.

"Shit's not going well, Prez. Not at all." Shatter was the first one to open his mouth.

I wanted to rip his beard off for stating the obvious. Hard to do that when it was absolutely fucking true.

"What's next?" Blaze asked. "The tattoo parlor? This clubhouse? Hell, maybe they'll roll right by and do a raid in North Dakota. The Snakes MC up in Canada are bitching about losing this shipment. This shit's gotta change. If our partners are getting restless, we're gonna lose –"

I slammed my fists on the table. "We fucking know it, brother!"

All eyes were on me. I'd let everybody express their concerns, but I wasn't letting anyone else make the decisions here.

"Look, they've gotten the drop on us – what? – three or four times now. Bastards are running fucking circles around us, hitting our income, and we can't hit theirs in this territory because we can't find them. Bastards are like ninjas on bikes."

There were a couple chuckles behind me. I let it go. Too fucking serious to bother giving a couple Dakota boys the evil eye.

"Blaze, you said something last night that I threw out like an idiot at the time. This isn't the same war this MC fought against them in Sturgis, or even against the Skulls last year. We're dealing with an enemy who'll keep doing hit and runs until their buddies show up. They're biding their time, waiting for reinforcements. Then they'll spring the trap. We've got to set one for them first."

Blaze's expression froze. My brother and VP probably couldn't believe I'd admitted he was right.

Wasn't fucking easy. Of course, coming up with the specifics was down to me, and I'd spent all damned morning thinking about it while I pretended to give a shit about the county's arson investigation.

"There's one way we *can* lure them out, but it means this club will have to do the unthinkable. And if it succeeds, then it needs to be total. Every last one of them better be dead, buried deep. Any leaks, any survivors, *will* cost us our reputation and our honor."

Everybody around me stood a little straighter, waiting with baited breath. I said the word.

"You can't do that! Are you fucking crazy!" Blaze led the room's explosion in violent protest.

I let the chatter fly back and forth, insults that would've meant I'd need to beat the ass of anyone who said those words to a club President in ordinary times.

These weren't fucking ordinary times. Far from it.

"You guys done?" I asked, pounding the table lightly with both fists for emphasis. "Every Devils' charter says this kinda shit goes up for a vote. I'll give you that, my brothers, but let me tell you this. I'd rather die than have us branded as despicable pussies, just like the rest of you, if this doesn't go the way I think. Only thing I'd like better is to have the other sorry bastards dead first."

"There's got to be another way..." Blaze muttered, running a tense hand through his thick hair.

I waited, along with everybody else. He didn't have a damned thing.

The plan was fucking crazy, and it was all we had because there wasn't a Plan B.

Nothing but retreat or going down fighting, and neither was too appealing when we still had a ghostly chance at shattering the Missoula Grizzlies.

"Nobody? Well then, let's vote. We'll start with you, Shatter, and go down the line…"

"Wake up, babe. I need you to get dressed and ready to run. This is a big day for all of us."

I shook June awake the next morning. She hadn't slept well either, the same as me. Probably all my shitty energy rubbing off on her.

My guts were still tangled in painful knots. Couldn't remember the last time that had happened. Probably not since I came back to Iowa to help Aimee. It hurt like hell knowing she was hooked on that crap, and I was afraid I'd find her dead when I pushed my way inside our old house.

Familiar rage and worry rippled through my system, like some nasty animal down my throat, clawing at my insides. Stroking June awake by the hair made things a tiny bit better. But only a little.

"Hmm? Aaron, what the fuck!"

The object I held out got her attention. She jerked up and pulled the sheets over her, protective and scared.

"You need to take this. I'd show you how to use it the right way, but we've run out of time. Take it, June. It's your last resort in case anything fucking crazy happens here."

Her hand shook a couple times, and then steadied. I held the razor sharp dagger out to her, and watched her soft fingers wrap around the handle.

"If anybody without a Prairie Devils patch lays a single finger on you, don't hesitate to jab it in his throat. Kill him, and run. You're welcome to do that now if you've changed your mind about staying – "

"No!" She shook her head vigorously, powerful sadness replacing the fear in her eyes. "This is the day it comes to a head, isn't it? I want to be around for this...I'm staying. Just like I promised."

Violent adrenaline shot through my heart. I had to shove back the caveman instinct to knock the knife out of her hands, put her on the back of my bike, and drive her far, far away from this fucked up place.

But she was hellbent standing her ground. And for all I knew, it was already too late.

The call I'd placed last night after the club's vote went my way was the hardest I had to make in my life. I sat through every slurred insult and nasty fucking chuckle coming out of Vulture's mouth on the other end of the line.

June threw herself into my arms. It should've been sweet, comforting, loving.

All I heard when I held her close were his words.

Sinister, sick, and evil.

Vulture's promise made me want to hunt and kill, instead of torturing myself by being patient. But I had to. Nothing else mattered except protecting the beauty wedged against my chest.

Prairie Pussies! You little cocksuckers get nothing if you're gonna go bitch. Do you hear me?

Nothing!

Keep your cunts warm for us tomorrow. We're coming, and we're gonna take everything from you. Everything.

We'll piss on your fucking colors and send you back East with your useless cocks between your legs.

Got it?

"Yes, sir."

Good sissy boy. Don't have any second thoughts now, Maverick. If anybody flashes a gun or raises their fist, I swear I'll kill every last one of you right in your own clubhouse.

Including the mopey little cunt we turned over as collateral. Keep your word, boy, or I'll shoot her in the fucking spine right in front of you.

"What's wrong? Can't you tell me anything, Aaron?" June felt me trembling unevenly as she clung to my embrace.

Fucking nerves. I clenched my jaw and flexed my muscles to steady myself, so hard I thought they'd break.

I wouldn't – couldn't – say a damned word.

"Let me guess…club business?"

"Damned right, babe. Whatever happens, I need you to know I love you, and this is a one-time deal. You never get to do this again. Having you in danger's killing me."

She cocked her head, uncertain what I meant. The pained expression on her face made me hold her tighter.

"Soon as this shit's done, I'm never, ever putting you in harm's way again. I'd rather die a thousand times first."

IX: Margin of Error (June)

My heart rode wild in my chest when I heard bikes roaring in. All the guys were gathered near the front, and I was behind the bar, exactly where Maverick told me to wait.

Something big, crazy, and terrifying was going on.

Nobody had said a word all morning. They just stood like soldiers near the front entrance, Maverick a little ahead of them. All their patches were turned toward me, a show of strength and also a creepy reminder that it hadn't been enough.

Not yet. The Grizzlies had the club by the balls, and I was scared they were about to rip them clean off.

The strange bikes by the garages. Men climbed off, walking toward the clubhouse.

No...

A familiar face came striding up to the door. Skinny, bearded, and filthy as ever. Vulture and his men streamed inside, and I slid down on the little chair, hiding as much as I possibly could behind the counter.

Now I understood why he'd given me the knife. I reached to my side and fingered it, wondering if I'd have to use it on myself.

Never. I shook my head, forcing myself to look at the man I hated as he squeezed my lover's arm. *I won't kill myself like Clara. I'll go down fighting instead, dying with everything I've got.*

The Presidents didn't shake hands as equals. Vulture grabbed at Maverick's forearm like he owned him, digging his dirty fingers into my love's beautiful tattoos.

"Shall we?" Vulture finally broke the handshake and waved to the big table in the center of the room.

It was the only one standing with all the others folded up or cleared to the sides. Ice nipped at my veins, but I wouldn't let it freeze me or make me sob. Not in front of them.

The Grizzlies lined up behind their leader, and the Devils did the same. Didn't look good that our guys were outnumbered two or three times.

God, the rival MC looked as disgusting and wicked as I remembered. Half their cuts were dirty, and some of the guys looked full on high, shifting their weight every few seconds to stay awake.

I couldn't believe these tweakers had caused so much damage. Then I remembered how they lived by brutality. Atrocities were just part of the game to them, the one thing distinguishing them from another one-percenter MC like the Prairie Devils.

They were dirty, ugly, and crude, but the Grizzlies were efficient. Experts in pain and fear.

"I won't waste time patting your boys down. There'll be plenty more humiliation to come," Vulture said with a smile. "First thing's first. I need you to turn over the nice little arsenal your buddies dropped off from out East."

Maverick's teeth appeared as he tensed his lips, holding in a snarl.

"Fine. I already told you, that's yours. Everything here, as long as you allow us safe passage out of here. With no reprisals."

"Everything?" Vulture cooed.

Hearing such a dangerous looking man talking like a grandpa playing coy sent chills up my back. I shook my head. Didn't want to draw attention to myself, but I couldn't fucking help it.

Jesus Christ, Aaron. What have you done?

"What else do you want?"

"The bikes. My club always needs a few extra hogs for riding, or for keeping on hand for scrap. Yours are a little newer than ours...gonna enjoy trying something a little more sleek and stylish."

Vulture grinned, intentionally looking past Maverick's cold expression. Behind him, his brothers looked like they were going to explode. Blaze craned his neck, staring halfway up at the ceiling, probably to keep him from jumping the asshole taunting and demanding everything.

"It's done. We agreed to that on the phone. I'll have my guys show yours the way right now."

Several Grizzlies started to move, walking toward the door. Vulture's arm shot up.

"No. We haven't gone over all the fine points yet. I have more demands." He paused, produced a cigarette from his pocket, and lit it. "Gotta keep my men here to make sure you boys don't do anything retarded. We've kicked your asses without our full force, but I'm not taking any chances. No more double crosses from the Prairie Pussies."

Vulture took a long drag on his cigarette. He held it out, intentionally flicking ash past the tray on the table. He blew it toward Maverick, against the PRESIDENT and 1% patches on his front.

Oh, fuck.

I waited for all hell to break lose. Maverick the President proved he could do bone shattering violence, a stern contrast to the loving guardian I knew as Aaron.

Any second, he'd throw a punch, or pick up Vulture and send his gross face spinning into the nearest table.

Wouldn't he?

I waited, and nothing happened. Maverick just brushed the ash off his cut and folded his hands, placing them on the table.

"That's fine. What else is it you want?" he asked coldly.

Vulture's eyes narrowed. Looked like he couldn't believe the man across from him was giving into all his troll demands. He'd already gotten everything that meant anything to an outlaw MC.

"Money. Supplies. All your profits from the strip club, plus the insurance pay out coming to you for scorching that fucking place to the ground." Vulture spread his hands on the table and leaned in close. "I don't give a fuck if the badge or the tax man busts your balls. They're you're problem. Getting us our fucking money is on your plate too."

"Whatever. We'll figure something out." Maverick pushed his chair back.

It was so damned silent in the clubhouse any noise was weirdly jarring. A Grizzlies goon scraped his boot on the floor.

I held my breath.

"Blaze, why don't you show these men outside to examine the bikes? You're gonna need a lot of help loading them up. Hope you brought a truck."

"Screw you, bitch. We're riding those fucking Harleys back to Missoula. Just turn over all the keys and don't waste our time. I'm not interested in letting your guys weep over their babies going bye-bye."

"If that's the way you want to do it…"

The Prairie Devils cleared a path for the Grizzlies as they walked past, making their way to the rear entrance toward the garages, where Blaze gestured.

"Hold up! Claws, get your ass over here." The rest of the men paused when Vulture yelled. "It's too fucking easy. We've done everything but piss on your colors – and believe me, that's coming after we take your cuts and fill ourselves on beer and whiskey. You got a problem with that, Maverick?"

"No."

Vulture looked pissed. Wasn't surprising he was a sore winner.

He folded his arms and looked around, reaching for another cigarette. I sank a few more inches behind the counter when he saw me, and the fingers fiddling in his pocket stopped.

"Hey...I got one more demand, boy." Vulture smiled, looking right at me and then turning back to Maverick. "Anything we gave up as collateral is ours. Isn't fucking fair you should keep it. I want her back."

He pivoted, pointing a knobby finger at me.

My mouth dropped. I saw Maverick jerk up taller, holding in a painful breath.

"That wasn't part of the deal...I'm giving you all our materials, bikes, and money. Lots of money. Colors are yours, and so is everything else that's worth a dime."

"We don't need your fucking money!" Vulture slammed his hands flat on the table so hard it shook. "We need you out of our territory, and we need payment for the blood you spilled. You fuckers killed Scoop, and that's gotta be paid in flesh. Except I'm not in the mood for man flesh."

Maverick's nostrils flared. He said nothing, but I saw his fists forming at his sides, ready to strike.

Vulture raised his hand. All the Grizzlies at the other end of the clubhouse reached into their pockets and produced guns, training them on all the outnumbered Devils, even on me.

"Is there a fucking problem here, man? Cause if there is, I can fix it with solid lead. I'm sure you got a few brooms in a dingy closet somewhere to sweep up all your pig blood after we're done with this, and I'll fucking take everything of yours anyway, including the girl."

Maverick swallowed hard. He never took his eyes off Vulture, and I sensed a line had been crossed.

Snarling, Vulture reached near his hip and pulled out a handgun. He stepped forward, until the gun was pressed on Maverick's forehead, ready to kill him in a blink.

"What's it gonna be? Think fast, bitch. My time's very valuable."

"Wait!" I screamed, ignoring two more guns shifting onto me.

I stepped out from behind the bar. Maverick and Vulture both looked at me.

I saw horror in my love's eyes. He shook his head so grimly I could practically hear the words, *No, babe! God damn it, no!*

"I'll do it. I'll give myself up. Just please – don't hurt him!"

Vulture squinted at me. After a second, he laughed, and lowered his gun. He walked toward me, footstep by painful footstep, and then stopped when he was behind me.

I smelled his reeking breath. His dirty fingers danced up my back, stopping at my ponytail. He seized it, pulled, and relished the sound I made when I squealed.

Revulsion and pain shot through my system. The complete opposite of everything I felt when Maverick touched me this way.

"Looks like we got ourselves a deal, boy!" I realized he was talking to Maverick. "Claws, make sure this pretty little thing doesn't wriggle away. Everybody else, get out there and check out those bikes. Let's get them out of here before we come back for all this other shit."

The Grizzlies stampeded down the hall and flung open the back door. They were like kids chasing after new toys. Two burly enforcers stayed behind to guard the small group of Devils. Maverick's men were cornered, eyes aimed at the ground, breathing fire in every shaky breath.

If I weren't deep in the putrid scent of the man I hated most, I would've felt some serious sympathy. Maverick looked numb. One look at his contorted face made me want to breakdown in tears.

"Where's your fucking room, bitch?" Vulture waited. No answer. "Don't make me ask again, or I'll re-think bringing this cunt to our clubhouse alive."

He jerked on my hair. I stopped a scream in my throat. It was hopeless, even with the knife, but I wasn't giving him any fucking satisfaction.

"Down the hall," Maverick whispered, barely audible.

"Come on!" He spun me around on my heels, jerking my hair violently. "You too, Claws. Bring our gracious host too. Been a long fucking time since I had fun with this baby girl. Oh, wait – that was her twin sister!"

His face darkened. "I just wish Scoop was here to enjoy this with me. Looks like I'll have to do the fuckin' for both of us."

Maverick took a quick step forward. Claws whipped out a gun and trained it on him, ordering him to follow.

My worst nightmare was coming true, three years late.

It should've torn what little was left of my soul away from me, but I felt a strange sort of calm. I'd never been religious. I just prayed there was some justice in the universe, and that I'd see Maverick again alive.

Somehow. Somewhere. If only I made it through this in one piece…

The door slammed behind us. We were in Aaron's room, next to the bed where I'd slept next to my love and enjoyed his gorgeous body so many times.

"Don't fucking do this," Maverick hissed.

Vulture stared at him, and Claws never moved the gun once. A rough, unwanted hand fondled my breast. My captor found my nipple and pinched hard.

I bit my lips shut, holding in the repulsive cry building in my body.

"Fuck. You're quiet now, but we'll figure out what lights your fire…" He looked up at Maverick. "Be grateful I'm letting you watch, bitch. It's the last time you're gonna see her alive. Maybe if you let her beg, I'll reconsider. Beg me, boy."

"Hands and knees," Claws chimed in, laughing like a cruel teenager.

Maverick dropped to the floor. He put his hands out, a terrible sadness raging in his bloodshot eyes, desperate like a feral animal.

"Do whatever the fuck you want to me. Just let her go. *Please.*"

Vulture's grip lessened. He took his hand off my breast and fixed his black eyes on my man.

"Hmm. Gotta say, that was pretty good, but not good enough. I changed my fucking mind!"

He ripped at my clothes, jerking me backward toward his vile erection. He forced himself against my ass, rubbing hard. One hand went to my breasts again, clawing and squeezing, and the other went straight down my pants.

When his dirty fingers touched me *there*, I lost it. I screamed.

"Shut up! Jesus, you really scream just like her, baby. If there's one thing I like fuckin', it's dumb sluts, but not when they're making my ears bleed. Took all those pills to shut up your sister's piggy squeals after we had our fun. Fuck, that's the only thing I remember about that cunt. That and how tight she was."

"What?" I started to shake.

"You didn't know?" he whispered, licking at my earlobe. "I finished her myself. Scoop held her down while I stuffed pills down her whore throat. Heh, everybody had a good laugh over your mopey ass. It was real fucking fun making you think she offed herself all these years...but we've both grown up. You haven't begun to see what real fun is, darlin'. You haven't seen a fraction of what I'm gonna do to you."

He grabbed my shoulders and pushed me down. Claws laughed behind me, and Maverick's rage came out in hot, heavy breaths I could hear through the silence.

Vulture's belt buckle clicked as his hands worked it away.

I was numb. Dizzy. Exhausted. This asshole had taken one horrific weight off my shoulders and replaced it with another, making rape and torture the price for truth.

Hot, confused tears blurred my eyes. I didn't even see his filthy cock clearly when he took it out, throbbing in his hand.

"Suck it. Don't make me suffocate your pretty ass. Your sis screamed like the fucking devil after I choked her on this dick, but I'm not taking those chances if you refuse." He wagged his finger at my forehead. "Hop to it. Take it good and maybe I won't have to – "

A sound like the sky rending apart swallowed the end of his sentence.

Everybody jumped in the room, and then jumped again when hail pounded on the roof, a steady shrapnel rain far bigger than chunks of ice. Vulture and Claws looked at one another, stupefied by the explosion.

Maverick and I locked eyes. A second later, he pounced, pushing Claws at the knees so fucking hard he slammed straight to the floor. The gun flew from his hands.

Before Vulture could react, I grabbed his cock. I pushed it away and reached for his balls, feeling for his clammy, wrinkly skin. When I found it, I clenched down hard, digging my nails in, crushing his degenerate sac in my hand.

Something rubbery popped and the waning hellfire on the roof was drowned out by his screams.

I squeezed again. And then again and again and again, annihilating his most vulnerable part, even as he tried to weakly slap my hand away.

I looked over as he fell. Maverick was on top of Claws, bashing his head into the wooden floor. The man was limp, his forehead nothing but a red mess.

My hand went for my pocket. I ripped the knife out of its holster and held it, shaking, hovering over the broken man writhing and moaning on the floor.

"Do it, June. You deserve this kill." Maverick was at my side, Claws' gun in his hands. "Put this fucking mad dog down. Doesn't have to be quick and easy."

Fury seethed in his eyes like shooting stars. If it were up to Maverick, he would've flayed the skin off Vulture's body, or done something so awful I couldn't even imagine it.

I had those fantasies. I imagined slowly torturing him alive, starting at his wrecked balls and working my way up...

This bastard had tormented me and taken up good air on this earth for too long. I came up to eye level with him, looking in his pain stricken eyes. For the first time ever, they weren't nasty or domineering.

They were frightened. I listened to his painful whimpering as he held what was left of his manhood.

"This isn't for trying to rape me or trying to kill the man I love," I said softly. "This is for Clara!"

I held the big knife in my fist and brought it down, stabbing him right in his throat.

His whole body lurched, bled, and seemed to go into a seizure. His death noises were sicker than I expected. I covered my ears and jumped away.

"It's over, babe. We fucking did it." Maverick picked me clean off the floor and squeezed me against his chest.

I laughed and cried simultaneously, loving the heat of his forehead against mine. God, I thought they'd stolen it from me forever.

Two gunshots burst out in quick succession through the wall. The faint scent of something burning hit my nose. His smile melted and he dropped me to my feet, running for the door.

"Stay here!" He shouted behind me.

Shit. We were so close to home free. I didn't have a clue what the hell had happened out there – a bomb? A firefight? An act of God?

Too curious for my own good, I slowly stepped out of our room where the two men lay dead. There were voices down the hall, but I couldn't make them out until I got closer.

"You're sure you got them all? A hundred percent? We need to fucking move, Blaze. Clock's ticking." Maverick's voice.

"Just finished the last two myself. Fuckers were flopping around like fish out of water. Everybody else was burned to a crisp in the explosion or killed."

I watched them, eyeing the gun in Blaze's hand.

"Round up the boys and let's get the hell out of here. It's a miracle this whole fucking place hasn't caught on fire yet. The cops won't be far behind after making this much commotion."

I saw Shatter blow right past them, carrying a big box of whiskey away from the bar. "I'm all set! There's room in the truck for a little celebrating."

Blaze and Maverick looked at each other and slowly grinned. It was oddly lighthearted for the complete chaos going on all around us.

He looked over, saw me, and waved his hand, gesturing me forward. I obeyed.

"Outside, babe. Right now. This whole fucking place is toast. We can't be caught here when the firetrucks and squad cars roll up."

Taking my hand, he led me outside, with Blaze right behind us. Stepping out the front entrance and around the corner, I saw the total hell that had been unleashed.

A mangled Harley dangled half off the roof. Broken bikes, little fires, and metal were scattered everywhere. Shit, and what was that awful smell?

I didn't have time to think about it.

Before I knew it, he shoved me into the truck, right next to Shatter's precious whiskey. Maverick started the engine and floored it, ripping out of the parking lot. The other vehicle, a big van brought over from the Dakota crew, had everybody loaded up too.

It trailed a little ways behind us with Blaze at the wheel.

My mind snapped. All the insane shit that had happened for the last hour registered, and it kicked harder than a shot of something strong and pure.

"What the fuck was it, Aaron? What did you do to them?" I gripped his bicep, above where his hand rested on the stick shift.

"Club business." He looked over at me, dead serious. Then he laughed.

I wrinkled my face and punched him. Not funny.

"Okay, maybe just this once, it's yours too…I knew surrendering would bring them all out in droves. The Prairie Devils have never out and out surrendered to anybody. Bastard like Vulture wouldn't pass up the chance to rub our faces in the dirt. He was a greedy fuck too."

"Yeah." He wasn't wrong about that in the slightest.

"Knew he'd go after the bikes. We just had to wait and get all his boys in one place. Had half our Harleys rigged with explosives, clean to the ignition. Soon as they started one of the bomb bikes, it was all over." His cute smile melted. "I'm just fucking thankful it happened when it did. A minute later…fuck, babe, I'm so sorry. I never, ever planned on letting him take you."

He reached for my hand. I gave it to him, savoring his protective warmth.

I squeezed back. I wouldn't let him beat himself up or take the fall. I was the one who refused to leave when he'd given me chance after chance.

I'd been stupid, stubborn. Thank God I hadn't truly had to pay the price.

It hurt that it took *this* to make me see how much he really cared – how deep his love for really was.

"It's okay," I said firmly. "I'm never gonna take your warnings for granted again. Just like I promised."

He looked at me, beaming happy and fierce at the same time. Reminded me what a beautiful contrast he was, and I smiled.

"You better not, babe. Told you I'd spank your pretty ass raw if you don't listen to me, old lady or no." He reached over and gripped my thigh.

Grinning, I pushed my hand over his. Having those big, rough hands on my flesh was always a happy feeling.

Best of all, now we could enjoy ourselves without keeping one eye behind our backs. At last, we were free.

He carried me into the little motel in Bozeman. Maverick had the savage look in his eyes, the need that wouldn't let him stop until it was completely sated.

Blaze parked the van next to our truck and his guys filed out. He started to say a few words, but Maverick wouldn't hear it, pushing past his VP.

"It'll wait. We'll touch base with Throttle and figure the rest out tomorrow. The worst is over, brother. Let's enjoy the fact we're all in one piece."

We went inside and checked into our room. Upstairs, he threw open the door, slammed it shut with his boot, and then pressed me to the wall.

Maverick's lips came heavy, fast, and fierce.

I moaned into his kisses, devouring his heat. His hands ran down my back, smoothing my sides. When they cupped my ass and squeezed, I stiffened, breaking the kiss.

"What's wrong?"

My heart was pounding.

He looked at me with an intensity unlike anything I'd ever seen in his deep, dark eyes. Then he realized what was happening.

"Don't think about that fucking rat…what he did to you. Think about me." He kissed me again. Harder. "Don't think, babe. Just feel. I'm gonna bury myself in you so deep tonight you won't ever be able to think about sex without seeing. You'll see me, feel me, and know I'm the only thing you'll think about. Nothing else."

I smiled as he came in for another kiss. Persistence paid off, and I was willing to try, even though my nerves resisted.

His tongue darted out, rough and conquering. It thrust past my lips, stroking me, softening me up for greater glories.

I sizzled when his hand brushed up my thigh. Maverick moved his fingers up slowly, stopping at my waist to curl down my pants. His fingers swept my panties aside and pushed their way into me.

Like magic, the nightmare broke, replaced with sultry desire.

Vulture's evil commands and sick face faded. My lover, my savior, flicked his thumb over my clit, oiling me in my own wetness. Every stroke replaced darkness with pleasurable light.

I threw my hands around his neck and pulled him in. His mouth kissed down my neck, and his free hand reached up to shove my shirt up, feeling for my breast.

"God!" I purred. "Aaron!"

He bristled at using his real name, but he never told me to stop. It seemed to energize him, as though he took joy in sharing a secret privilege he didn't give to anybody else.

Aaron. Maverick. Whoever and whatever you are, I love you.

And I love your fucking body too.

Growling, he tore himself away from me. Maverick picked me up off the floor again and made a straight line for the bed.

"Better get your clothes off, babe. If you don't take care of them now, I won't be able to stop myself from tearing off the wrapper to get what's mine."

"I'm not a candy bar!" I said jokingly, brushing my cheek on his stubble.

His edges were rough, yeah, but they always felt *very* fucking good.

"Maybe you ought to be. I'm gonna savor every inch of you tonight. Come to think of it, I don't know many candy bars begging to be filled. You want it bad, don't you?"

Before I could answer, he dropped me on the bed. I didn't use my words. I used my hands, rolling up my shirt and popping my bra in record time.

He watched the whole time as I yanked off my clothes and tossed them on the floor. He didn't join me until I was fully naked, inviting, and spread for him.

"Play with your clit and watch me, babe. I want you wetter than fucking rain when I get between your legs."

Shit, another first. I'd never rubbed myself in front of a man before. He once again made me do the unthinkable, leading me to virgin territory I'd never explored.

If there was one thing I'd learned by now, it was to trust him with my very being. I rubbed one hand up and down my slit, moaning when I discovered just how wet I was.

Maverick smiled at his good work. Slowly, he raised his arms and dropped his cut, then dragged the shirt underneath up over his head, inch by throbbing inch.

Was this what it felt like when guys watched porn? My lust went up another notch when I saw his bare, muscular chest in all its tattooed, flaming, screaming glory. When he dropped his pants and tugged down his boxers, his cock popped out, angry and ready.

He pumped it twice in his fist, drowning me in fresh intensity.

"Oh!" I almost came, circling my clit faster and faster. "Don't torture me like this. Fuck me so hard I won't ever forget this night."

He didn't need to be asked twice. The bed sank fast beneath his weight and he was on me like a tiger, shoving my legs apart.

I wasn't a small gal, but he managed to fit them up over his shoulders, and it wasn't uncomfortable. He sank into me, groaning like he'd just tasted the best thing in the world.

Dig in, I thought. *I'm your feast tonight. Every fucking inch of me. Just like you said.*

I want you to have your fill, Maverick. Be a glutton.

His cock sank up and wedged against my womb. Then he pulled back, faster, before slamming into me again, all the way up to the hilt.

Then it was just straight on fucking. He growled and jerked his hips, leveling himself deeper than he'd ever been before with his massive cock, hitting new angles that made me writhe beneath him.

Ten thrusts in and I came, convulsing around the steady slap of his balls on my flesh. Wet heat flooded me, pouring all over his cock, tightening around him like a vice.

I screamed. The paper thin walls in this cheap motel wouldn't keep out anything.

For all I knew, his brothers were in the other rooms next to ours, listening as he ravished me like the property I was. The idea wasn't strange or embarrassing.

I wanted the whole world to know I'd given myself to this man. He owned me now, total and complete, and my body reacted to him like nobody else.

"Fucking tight and wet, babe! Keep clenching your sweet cunt around me." He drove on, hips moving like a piston.

His deep strokes wouldn't even let me come down from the insane heights. I was jettisoned into outer space, where everything was full of stars and white hot ecstasy.

My clit throbbed a steady tempo. At some point, he reached down and stroked it, adding to my fire. I was already far too burned to keep track.

I thought he was on the verge of coming, but suddenly the thrusting stopped. He held himself in me, slowly swiveling his hips, tracing my face with one rough hand.

"You thinking about anything but this, babe?" He thrust hard and deep several times.

I cried out, clenching the sheets. "No! Oh my God – no! *Please.*"

"Good girls get what they deserve. Come with me, June. Come like a motherfucking firecracker."

He bared his teeth and grabbed my legs, holding them high, thrusting down into me. The bed shook like it was about to break.

Nice to know we could make the springs sing anywhere, even if his old bed where we'd first made love was gone forever.

Aaron jerked one more time and stopped, groaning like a bull. His cock swelled as my sex clenched. We exploded together, cascading pleasure through our bodies.

Nothing else mattered here, wrapped so snug and tight around him as he filled me with his seed. Nothing but this.

Not the old demons, finally vanquished for good. Not the uncertainty about whatever the hell the future held.

In this space, it was just him and I. Sweating, grunting, and twitching in a rhythm so intense it wiped me clean.

Maverick pulled out and left behind a steaming flow between my legs. I rolled, making room for him, smiling when he encircled me in dark inked muscle.

"You really think everything's going to be all right now?" I asked him the question I'd been afraid to ask since we left the shattered clubhouse.

I needed to know. MC life would never be easy and normal, old lady or not, but surely it would be calmer than this going forward. I was willing to ride the choppy waters, as long as it was with him, steering us away from the big storms.

"Babe, I know it will. I've done my job for mother charter, though Throttle isn't gonna like the way it came down. I'm a Nomad, June, and you're a Nomad's old lady. Soon as our shit's in order, we can go anywhere we want. Well, anywhere there's a Prairie Devils clubhouse in fifty miles."

"Really?" It honestly excited me.

"Really," he repeated. "Study the map while I'm taking care of business. We'll take a long run this summer, wherever you want."

I'd never lived anywhere except Western Montana. Knowing we were truly free to start over anywhere we wanted was exhilarating, strange, and scary all at once.

"I'll have to give it some thought. When will you and the guys get new bikes?" It was strange to have the whole MC reduced to using trucks and vans.

"Soon as fucking possible." It was exactly what I thought he'd say. "Dunno when, but I don't really care. Harleys come and go, even though I love 'em to death. I'd rather have you riding on the back and in my bed any day – that's what's really important."

He turned toward me and smiled. Those had to be the sweetest words a biker could ever say to an old lady.

"I love you," I whispered.

"Love you, babe." Growling, he pulled me close, kissing me with a rougher fury. "You and that sweet ass of yours are gonna be with me until the day I die."

Laughing, I took his kisses one by one, relishing the feel of his new erection stiffening between us.

X: Bitter Peace (Maverick)

There were fifty guys wearing the full Prairie Devils patch in the old barn. Pretty damned big group for us, but they were bigger.

The Grizzlies had at least a hundred bikers. They flanked the other side of the barn, standing like soldiers, ready to turn this war from cold to hot at a moment's notice.

"Come on, Maverick. You're with me. This is our business." I followed Throttle as he stepped away from our group. Our counterparts on the other side did the same.

It was a big, tall guy with a cut fully decked in patches. The Grizzlies went overboard, especially for Fang, President of their mother charter in Sacramento.

Old Ursa was at his side, the Missoula President who'd let his club go to hell by pushing shit off on his VP. And he'd paid for it dearly by losing the whole charter.

"Let's get this over with. It's a long fucking ride to North Dakota," Throttle said, stopping at the worn table in the middle of the room.

"Long ass ride to Cali too," Fang said. "Makes me want to break out the guns and kill all you assholes so I never have to drag my ass up here again."

Throttle smiled. "Go ahead and try. My club will survive further east without a head. Can't say the same for you with the cartels nipping at your heels down south."

Fang frowned. He looked at me, and then at Ursa. I stared like a rock. Didn't want to let on anything I was thinking to these bastards.

"I'd be real careful about the bets you're making, boys. You've both been awful lucky. One of these days, your gamble's gonna go the other way. Your whole MC's gonna pay big time. Blood and cash." Fang looked us up and down, his hand a couple inches from his pocket.

Shit. If he was going for his side-arm now to start some shit, nobody could stop it. With this many guys, the bullets were judge, jury, and executioner. Even orders from MC heads didn't matter once the party started with this many bikers invited.

"Listen, it seems to me we're at an impasse." Throttle leaned forward, and Fang's hand stopped its slide toward his pocket. "Truth is my brother here kicked all your asses, even though they were outnumbered and outgunned. Only trouble is we can't move further West. I know when I've had a lucky break. I'm not so crazy I'll push into your territory, Fang. Hell, we can't have a proper clubhouse in Python anytime soon after all the attention over this shit."

"Too bad!" Fang spat. "If you mean you Devils got your way by trickery and double crosses, you're right."

"Little reminder," I spoke up. "Ursa's club double crossed us first. They sent vulnerable guys into our businesses to scope things out after we made our little agreement. Then when we tried to solve things peacefully, he bit off more than he could chew. Nobody fucking takes back a girl when she's my old lady."

Fang spun around, laughing, making a full 360 before looking at Throttle and I again.

"You guys are really fucking serious, aren't you? Holy mother of hell! You think I'm an idiot." His voice darkened, low and menacing. "Nobody fucking believed you were really gonna give yourself up without a fight. If old Vulture had any brains, he would've seen it coming."

"What's done is done," Throttle said loudly. "We can piss our time away talking about the past, or we can look toward the future."

"I don't see any future that doesn't involve me ordering my guys to put a bullet through every Devils' patch they find," Fang said coldly.

"That's where you're wrong. Trust is a hard thing to come by between our clubs – as it damned well should be. So, I'm gonna make you one more offer." Throttle cleared his throat. "We've got our supply route through Missoula now that your charter there's gone. But it isn't hitting our main market. Your club can't do shit up in Canada because you made some powerful enemies there."

"Fuck Canada!" Fang roared. "We do our business in the States and south of the border. All better markets than the frozen shithole where your friends live."

"Except the cartels aren't making things so easy anymore, are they? Wouldn't you like a cut of what's going through a border that isn't reaching down to bite your dick off?"

Fang looked at us both, narrowing his eyes. Ursa shuffled next to him. It was easy to tell the old President without a club wasn't liking where this was heading.

"And how the hell are we supposed to get a piece of that?"

"Give us Missoula. We set up a charter there, we won't move further West, and we'll have a sweet supply line straight up into Vancouver." Throttle paused. "Only if you give us free access, of course."

"Fine. Fifty-percent cut plus a fifty big starter fee. You fuckers take your colors off when you hit the Idaho border, and don't put them back on until you get to Canada."

Throttle shook his head. "Twenty-percent, forty big starter, and everybody keeps their colors."

"Fang! What the fuck?" Ursa tugged at his sleeve like an insolent little boy. "You let all my men die for nothing?"

Very slowly, Fang turned to the old man at his side. "You don't got a fucking club anymore, gramps. Now shut up before I send you to the retirement home instead of somewhere warmer."

Ursa stared at me hatefully. I grinned, quickly flashing my smile, and then hiding it just as fast when the two Presidents started up again.

"Forty-percent, fifty big, and no god damned colors. We're not sneaky fucking pushovers like you assholes. You wanna ride through our territory, with our blessings, then show some fucking respect!" Fang looked slapped the table like a gorilla.

"Last offer," Throttle said quietly. "Thirty-five – right where we both know this is gonna end. Forty big, plus an extra ten in damages. We keep our colors, but we'll fill up in Coeur d'Alene and ride all the way through to Vancouver. No Devil will stop in a single Washington bar for beer or pussy. Only time you'll see us is when somebody comes by your Seattle clubhouse to drop off your money."

Fang stood tall, shook his head, and sighed. Next to him, Ursa was quietly fuming. I thought he'd have a stroke when the big boss extended his hand to Throttle.

They shook, each man trying to get a tighter, more dominant squeeze than the other.

"Don't fuck me on this, Throttle. You do, and I won't even hesitate to send my guys after you. I'll put a fucking price on your head and every Prairie Devils' President across the country."

Throttle smiled, ignoring the threat. "No need. I'm glad we could work shit this way instead of using lead."

I pressed my hands to my sides. The gun near my hip was still there, cold and ready for use. For once, using it didn't feel inevitable, though, and that was a relief.

"Whatever. Let's get the fuck out of here." Fang turned, heading back toward his guys, and we did the same.

The war was over. It defied all sense, history, and the fucking odds, but we did it. We won.

Blaze and I broke away from the main group on the way back to our temporary camp in Bozeman. My brother drove, I was in the passenger seat, and all three of my full patch guys plus five Dakota boys were in the back.

Felt like some kinda god damned family outing. It was good to see Tank with us again. He still looked a little pale, but he was up and moving with a shitty smile on his face.

Luckiest man in our MC. He took a bullet to dodge bombs in the clubhouse, and now he was getting a pretty new ride.

We headed for the dealership with a blank check from the club to pick up our new bikes.

The salesmen gave us the respect we deserved. It was extra nice seeing him slur his words and trip over a few more bulk discounts. I didn't doubt the man had dealt with outlaw MCs before.

News about what happened in Python must've made it here. The Prairie Devils weren't to be fucked with, and now our 1% patch meant something deadly fucking serious in this state.

With Missoula secured, our core business would be there. Not that we'd leave Python behind forever. Hoped to have a strip club there again next to the tattoo parlor one day. Least for now our dancers could relocate to the new joint in Missoula.

With the Grizzlies fucked, the Dirty Diamond was closing down further north. Devils owned and operated skin shops would soon be the only game in town.

I'd just mounted my new bike – a sleek baby with state of the art leather seats and some built in GPS shit – when my phone rang.

"Aaron? I haven't heard from you in weeks. What the hell have you and Michael been up to?"

"Planning a trip east, Sis. At least I am. Not sure about Blaze."

She giggled. Aimee thought the road names were silly.

Whatever, it was her right as a civilian, just as long as she respected them anywhere that mattered.

"You mean you're done fucking around out there in the mountains? Seen any bears yet?"

Not the kind you'd want to see in a zoo, Sis.

"Nothing. Haven't spent much time camping up in Glacier. I need to get back to the clubhouse. Somebody's waiting for me, plus Blaze and I really need to wrap this Montana shit up."

"Somebody? Is it the girl Michael told me about?" Her voice crackled with fascination.

Fuck. Blaze usually told me when he talked to our sister, but sometimes things slipped by.

Only one way to make this easy...

"Sure is." I decided to come clean. "Her name's June. You'll meet her soon, Aimee. For real. Got a good feeling we'll be swinging through Iowa sometime this summer."

"I can't wait! She's got to be amazing to hold her own with the big, gruff biker Prez, right? Talk to you later, bro."

"Later."

I cut the call. A little razzing aside, those were the calls I liked to have with my sister. She was sharp, and didn't sound the least bit strange in the little game of give and take all siblings play. Told me she was staying clear of the old world.

The new bike revved to life like a rocket beneath me. Most beautiful thing in the world, short of knowing the two women in my life were happy and healthy.

We took a long, slow ride through the mountains to the lodge where we were camping out. The new rides took a little getting used to. They were sleek, efficient, and razor sharp in the right hands. All that mattered to me.

I walked through the lodge's door with my boys behind me. A few hung back, caressing their pretty new rides like the bikes were the sweetest whores they'd ever gotten their hands on.

I was surprised to see Throttle standing just a few feet inside. He looked up when I stopped in front of him.

The world went blurry. He grabbed me by my cut, whirled me around, and sent his fist flying at my jaw.

Pain exploded in my brain, and again when I hit the floor hard. I licked my split lip and tasted blood. My brothers stood out of the way. Nobody was stupid enough to get between two beasts on top of the food chain.

"Get up, brother." Throttle extended a hand.

I took it, steadying myself and sucking more blood into my mouth. We looked at each other, nodded slowly, sharing an understanding only meant for two guys in real brotherhood.

"I know, I fucked up. You gonna take my bruise as an apology?" I said.

"Yeah, I am. Goes without saying you better never do anything as reckless and fucking crazy as what you did in Python without clearing it by me first. I'd tell you there'd be more consequences if shit went bad, but then if it had, we wouldn't be having this conversation at all."

I smiled. He was damned right about that.

"Church. Right now. Round up all the full patch members."

"You got it," I told him happily.

We were all crammed into the tiny meeting room, over two dozen guys from all the charters hanging out in Montana. Throttle and I shared the head of the table.

Technically, this was still my territory. But not for long if everything went well.

"As you all know, Fang and the Grizzlies took the deal. The Western front's more secure than it's ever been." He paused – master of fucking drama. "Let's make some god damned money!"

Brothers slapped each other's backs and cheered. We would've easily gotten a noise warning if this were any other hotel. Good thing the elderly owner was still one of us, even if he was way too old to ride and sport his colors.

"I've got a motion for everybody here," I said. "I think it's time to reinstate the Nomads. We came out here to plant Devils seeds on Western ground, and it's succeeded. We've done our jobs, haven't we, Throttle?"

He looked at me and quirked an eyebrow. "Yeah, I guess you have, brother. Had a feeling you wouldn't wait a minute longer to get the fuck back on the open road."

I grinned. Throttle shifted his gavel in hand, the original one used by his father and founding President, Voodoo.

"Well, let's get this over with. Everybody in favor of turning out the Nomads and electing officers for the new Missoula charter, say 'aye.'"

He went down the line. Ayes rang out, one by one, without pause. Unanimous.

The gavel came down. Throttle looked at me, and then at the rest of us.

"It's finished, brothers. Take my congratulations and hit the road whenever you're ready. If nobody has anything else, I think we can – "

"Hold up!" Blaze shouted, several seats over. "I want to change my patch permanently."

My eyes went wide and I stared at my brother in shock. What the fuck was happening here?

"I've worn the VP patch for the Nomads proudly, right beside my brother Maverick." He turned to me. "Thing is, I like it here. This latest shit with the Grizzlies reminds me I've been on the road for too long. I'm ready to trade a little freedom for the right to kick back in the same town, the same clubhouse. If there's no objection, I'd like to join the new Missoula charter."

Blaze and I shared a long, intense look. Hypno, Shatter, and Tank stared right along with me. Slowly, I nodded to him, giving him my blessing.

Blaze could be a real asshole, but he always came to his senses. He'd been a good VP and a good blood brother. I wasn't sure what the hell had gotten into him, but if he wanted this, then I wasn't gonna stand in his way.

The vote was swift. I said my 'aye,' without wavering for a second.

The second vote Throttle called was even more surprising. It passed just as easily, giving my brother a post he seriously deserved.

Not only was Blaze patched into the Missoula charter – it's first official member – he was patched in as President.

I got out of my chair and gave my brother a big, manly hug. Our father had been in an MC out East, before the Devils' time. He never would've believed both his sons would grow up to be Presidents in a club that commanded mad respect.

"Congratulations, brother. Now you get to take all the blame for other people's fuckups, just like me."

He laughed and returned my hug. The rest of the guys clapped and hollered. It was rare to have big church sessions like this between clubs, and now it had turned into something truly unusual.

"Okay! We've got fucking food and whiskey coming in as we speak out there. If nobody has anything else, we can work out Missoula's logistics later." Throttle was about to pound the gavel when Tank stood up.

"You remember me, boss. I was doing a lot of thinking while I was flat on my ass, and I've decided I'd like to stay in Missoula too."

I raised an eyebrow, but honestly wasn't as shocked by Tank's decision. Just didn't think it would be so public.

I saw the way he was making goo-goo eyes at Emma while she tended his wounds. Throttle looked at me, feeling me out, and I nodded.

"Let's vote."

Third vote, unanimous again. Hoped it was the last. The hungry looks on other faces said I wasn't the only one getting fucking tired of going around to this many guys.

"All right, brothers! Is there *anything* else?"

A couple guys snickered, but nobody stood up or raised their voice. Throttle brought the hammer down, and I was the first one rushing out the door, ready to meet up with June and party.

Fuck, it had been way too long since we had a good time.

June sat at the bar with another woman I recognized. Throttle's old lady.

They clinked glasses as I approached. Something about that made me smile. It told me she hadn't just gotten used to my brothers and I, but she was really getting into club life, mingling with old ladies and accepting her place.

Beautiful. Things are finally moving in the right direction.

"Hey, babe." I ran a possessive hand over her shoulder. Damn, she looked as good as she smelled tonight.

"You boys finally done in there? I think we were running out of girl talk waiting for you all to finish so we could break out the goods." Rachel razzed me with her words and her tongue.

"Girl talk? What the fuck's that?"

June squeezed my hand. "Pretty important, Maverick. My new friend was just telling me all about what I should expect now that you're my old man."

"Yeah? What sorts of things are those?" My hand slid all the way down her, until I covered her thigh.

Oh, hell. My cock was ready to skip the party and take her up to our room right now. I'd have to make the greedy bastard wait, though, because tonight was my last chance to see some brothers for a long time.

"It's old lady business!" Rach piped up in a girlish, sing-song voice. "Sorry. We don't talk about things like that with guys who aren't in our club."

I laughed. Blaze came up to me with an empty glass and a bottle of Jack. Pried my hands away from June's sweet curves just long enough to say hello.

Throttle slid behind the bar and wrapped an arm around his old lady's waist.

"Let's get to it, baby girl," he said, though he was also addressing all of us. "Can't leave our baby upstairs with the sitter forever."

June and I both smiled at him, and then we looked at each other. Didn't take a fucking psychic to know we were thinking the same thing.

Throttle and Rach had a damned good thing going, and in them, we saw our future. Probably approaching us a hell of a lot faster than it seemed.

Those moment's when everything's absolutely fucking perfect are rare in this life. That night, drinking, eating, and laughing our asses off, was definitely one of them.

When it was all over, I stumbled upstairs with my babe, and laid her out in the shower. She was wet *all over* and so fucking irresistible my whole body trembled, starting at my cock.

I pushed her naked, slick body against the wall and plowed into her. I never came so fucking fast after drinking in my life, and she did too.

Holy fuck. Didn't know what the hell this sweet girl was doing to me, but I liked it.

Must've been witchcraft, or some shit, because it was just getting better every single time I we did it.

Later, blissfully spent in bed, I cuddled her close. She still looked damned good pressed up naked around my tats. Didn't matter if my cock had its fill until morning.

"Did you study that map?" I asked.

She smiled sweetly and held my finger gently. "Yeah. How about Chicago? I always wanted to see a big city. Just once."

"Wherever you want, babe. We've got ourselves a clubhouse a little ways West of there. We'll stop through Iowa first, then circle down and hang out as long as you want."

"Iowa? What's there except corn fields?" She looked confused. Amazed it didn't do a damned thing to dent how sexy she looked.

"Got a sister I'd like you to meet. I know you lost your family," I said softly. "You've met most of mine in this MC. Just one more left to meet. Aimee's gonna love you."

She smiled, looking up at me with those damned enchanting eyes. The sadness was all gone, replaced by stars that were bright and warm. Didn't seem possible, but it made her look even more beautiful.

We kissed, and I looked forward to getting on the open road.

Everybody was on the move the next morning. Guys from all the charters dragged their asses, including me.

June and I shook off our hangovers with lots of water and some breakfast. Blaze sat across from me the whole time, wearing his cut with the new PRESIDENT patch already stitched on. He hadn't gotten his Missoula bottom rocker yet, but it wouldn't be far behind.

We laughed and said our goodbyes. He told me he'd call when we got to Aimee's place, and I made damned sure he better live up to his word.

Everybody from the Dakota crew and the Nomads pulled out together, with Throttle's and his boys riding lead.

Hypno and Shatter were behind me in perfect formation. Those two were vying for VP slot now that Blaze was gone – not that being VP meant much in a tiny Nomad charter with three guys.

We'd be looking for prospects in the Midwest, where the Prairie Devils always needed more guys. I looked forward to it, making a clean start, living like a Nomad again.

June leaned into me as we roared on through Montana beneath the big blue sky. She clinked her helmet gently on mine every so often, scratching my neck or teasing me with those sweet lips.

If she thought I was tired after last night, she had another thing coming.

Up ahead, Throttle's big convoy looked like tiny dots, heading back to Cassandra. Wouldn't be long at all until we went our separate ways.

The bright sun filled my eyes, and the air had the mild, sweet scent of the plains changing from spring to summer. June's hands gripped my waist tighter, feeling up my waist, anchoring me to what really mattered on this crazy fucking ride.

I wouldn't be a Nomad forever. Or at least not one with as much freedom as I craved, able to take off and go roaring across the country whenever the club wasn't calling in its troops.

When we were stuck in Python, I'd missed this, and it felt damned good to be free.

But as I enjoyed each and every one of her loving strokes, I knew the future would be perfect, no matter what happened. Sacrificing a little freedom to settle down somewhere and have kids with the woman I loved sounded pretty fucking good right about now.

I was ready. Just as long as June was at my side, an old lady as wild and free as my own heart.

Thanks!

Want more Nicole Snow? Sign up for my newsletter to hear about new releases, subscriber only goodies, and other fun stuff!

JOIN THE NICOLE SNOW NEWSLETTER! - http://eepurl.com/HwFW1

Thank you so much for buying this ebook. I hope my romances will brighten your mornings and darken your evenings with total pleasure. Sensuality makes everything more vivid, doesn't it?

If you liked this book, please consider leaving a review and checking out my other erotic romance tales.

Got a comment on my work? Email me at nicolesnowerotica@gmail.com. I love hearing from my fans!

Kisses,
Nicole Snow

More Erotic Romance by Nicole Snow

KEPT WOMEN: TWO FERTILE SUBMISSIVE
STORIES

SUBMISSIVE'S FOLLY (SEDUCED AND RAVAGED)

SUBMISSIVE'S EDUCATION

SUBMISSIVE'S HARD DISCOVERY

HER STRICT NEIGHBOR

SOLDIER'S STRICT ORDERS

COWBOY'S STRICT COMMANDS

RUSTLING UP A BRIDE: RANCHER'S PREGNANT
CURVES

FIGHT FOR HER HEART

BIG BAD DARE: TATTOOS AND SUBMISSION

OUTLAW KIND OF LOVE

SEXY SAMPLES: OUTLAW KIND OF LOVE

"Romance, huh? Didn't realize you were such a bookworm."

"Just something to keep the mind busy. I like to read, but it isn't my favorite thing in the world."

Jack was only inches away from me. I stared up into his big dark eyes. They completely sucked me in until I was lost in them. He left me awestruck, strangely curious about all the mysteries wrapped around this beautiful man.

"I had a feeling you'd say that, baby girl." He pushed his forehead against mine, stamping my lips with his hot breath. "Reading's no substitute for the real thing. Aren't you curious what a real man is like?"

Holy sh*t, holy sh*t...

My brain just shut down. His hands went to my low back, and then sank lower. He cupped my ass and squeezed, pulling me into him.

The bulge tenting the middle of his jeans pressed close. Sweat sizzled on my brow. I temporarily forgot how to breathe.

"I'm curious, yeah. Especially if that man is you."

I lifted my eyes slowly to his. Hunger steamed in the stars lining his pitch black pupils, tiny pinpricks as sharp and hot as lust itself.

"Don't you wonder any longer, Rach. Let me show you…"

He moved in for a kiss. I thought I was ready, but nothing truly prepared me for the hot, wet bliss of his wandering lips.

I moaned into his mouth, louder when his hands tightened on my ass. Jack kissed me deep, winding his tongue with mine, moving his lips in a steady, hypnotic pulse on my little inexperienced lips.

Excitement boiled up, bright and hot and addictive.

Through my daze, I noticed he was pushing me toward the bed, stopping to gently tap his knees on my legs when I reached the edge. He broke his kiss, sliding his calloused hand over my face, pouring more humid breath onto my cheeks behind it.

"F*ck. I can't wait any longer, baby girl. Let me unwrap you so we can do this thing. I've wanted to get you naked and tangled since the second I laid eyes you…"

More kisses. I was shaking in his arms, but he steadied me, a mountain of a man growing hotter by the nano-second.

His hands edged my shirt, lifting up. He rolled it halfway to my breasts, exposing my naked skin pocked with goosebumps.

I froze. There was something I had to tell him, before he really rendered me speechless.

"Wait. Wait, wait…there's something you need to know." I swallowed hard.

I didn't want to tell him and expose my immaturity. But this rock hard man deserved to know what he was getting by taking me as a lover, even if it meant he might not want me at all.

But men like virgins, right? I hoped everything I heard was true. Like, really, *really* f*cking hoped, sending a silent prayer up high.

"I've never done this before, Jack. I'm a virgin."

The smile on his face melted. It scared me at first, but that deeper, much hotter heat on his skin didn't lie. It was like his body temperature had gone up a few degrees.

Would he burst into flames and take me with him? God, I wanted him to.

"No f*cking way." He shook his head.

"Are you serious?" He ran his hand to my jawline and stopped, spreading it to hold my chin.

"I wouldn't lie to you." I nodded, loving the raw masculine feel of his palm on my softness.

"Baby girl, you just made my day, my week, my whole f*cking year. I'm gonna teach you so much, and it's gonna be amazing…"

Don't miss Jack and Rach's story in the first Outlaw Love book!

Look for Outlaw Kind of Love at your favorite retailer!